"Which of you is Lady Frome?"

"Why, I am," replied Harriet, too amazed to resent the rather hectoring tone in which the question had been asked.

"Then I must beg you to desist from involving my half-brother in your affairs. He has," she added, lifting her hand imperiously to forbid any interruption, "enough unpleasant, indeed one might almost say nefarious or unsavoury, affairs of his own to keep him wholly occupied!"

Harriet experienced a series of emotions, but cold fury triumphed. She said spacing her words, and, with such disdain as to rivet all eyes upon her, "If you will do me the courtesy of giving me your name, and that of your half-brother, I might, madam, be better able to comprehend you!"

But even as she spoke, Harriet suspected what the answer to her question would be. She felt a frisson of apprehension. But no one could ever make her deny her friendship with Hugh de Brandon. . . .

Fawcett Crest Books
by Joan Mellows:

FRIENDS AT KNOLL HOUSE

HARRIET

HARRIET

A Novel of Early 19th-Century England

BY

Joan Mellows

A FAWCETT CREST BOOK

Fawcett Publications, Inc., Greenwich, Connecticut

HARRIET

A Fawcett Crest Original

© 1977 FAWCETT PUBLICATIONS, INC.
ALL RIGHTS RESERVED

ISBN 0-449-23209-3

Printed in the United States of America

10   9   8   7   6   5   4   3   2   1

HARRIET

CHAPTER I

Although no longer in her early twenties, Harriet looked younger now than she did then. Her pretty figure, certainly, remained the same, although perhaps a little less rounded (and therefore less matronly), but it was in her countenance that the real change could be remarked. Where before her regard had been pleasantly open but speculative, a little concerned, the look perhaps of a young matron, or even an unfortunate young widow with heavy responsibilities of family and affairs to control, now she appeared gay, wholly happy, the soft brown eyes fringed with their thick lashes clear, untroubled, lively, and full of interest in everything about her. Her face had filled out a little, the slight, worried frown-lines vanished for good. Her hair, which formerly had seemed confined, the shimmering tendrils often hidden beneath a lace cap too old for her years, could now be seen in all its thick brown-gold beauty, controlled still, but with deliberate art, the fashion of a woman aware of her own beauty. In short, in both appearance and manner Harriet had improved beyond belief: without loss of her innate niceness of mind and affectionate nature, she had shed her air of motherly competence (often mistaken by many for autocracy), and now appeared as a creature not irresponsible, but carefree, intelligent, and charming.

Poor Harriet; until a little short of a year ago, except for a brief period of married happiness, she had had little enjoyment in life, and less chance of finding any. At seventeen, she had become companion and nurse to an ailing mother, and cipher to an autocratic, bluff father, who took little notice of his wife, and bothered not at all with his daughter unless some slip in the smooth running of his household, causing inconvenience to himself, occurred. That this is a frequent state of affairs for many unfortunate eldest, or only, daughters cannot be denied. But Harriet had felt a further responsibility as protectress of her young brother, a slender, sensitive youth some three years her junior. Sir Timothy Catesby had little use for his son, a dreamer, seemingly without the force or will to achieve much in any field. Certainly Geoffrey rode and shot well, and later acquired the requisite social graces, but aimlessly, without object or direction; worse, he read and wrote poetry, and had an extreme fondness for music, a state of affairs his father could neither understand nor tolerate. There was ever friction between them, and where Harriet, more practical, could to some extent see the lack of staying power in her brother, and sometimes deplore it, she felt much of the blame rested on their father's shoulders, who never, at any time, attempted to understand his son's artistic interests, or encouraged a determined pursuance of his more active ones. Faced with such a situation, she became the mother, and in household affairs, the wife, that the ailing Lady Catesby had never been.

Certainly, for two years Harriet had enjoyed a brief respite of happiness in her marriage to Lord Frome, a man of gentle and kindly nature some ten years older than herself, who realized the treasure she was, and loving her dearly, took her family responsibilities firmly on his own shoulders. And as these responsibilities were soon further lightened by the death of her papa, characteristically in the hunting field, and her mamma, some few months later, conveniently on her chaise longue, leaving only her brother as a charge upon her husband, life seemed set fair for the future.

But this was not to be. Lord Frome, never robust, died of a chill followed by a fever, and with his death, Harriet's responsibilities came crowding back on her. For a time, inconsolable, she visited friends, and, not lacking for sense, made a determined effort to avoid involvement in her brother's affairs, which became increasingly more demanding. Geoffrey having succeeded to his father's title and estates, there was no lack of money, but he was ever in some scrape or other, usually involving feminine company, for which he had developed a considerable fondness, and to whom his handsome fair looks and address were nigh irresistible. This might not have been so disturbing if he had trifled with ladies of the Town, but his interests lay in the daughters of his peers, and although at this stage never passing beyond the bounds of discretion, this trifling caused many small heartbreaks and awkwardnesses.

Despite all her efforts, however, he began frequently to

visit his sister during her early widowhood, asking her to return to her family home—to run it for him, she suspected, as some kind of chaperon, since his bachelor state sometimes made the pursuance of what might vulgarly be termed his hobby somewhat difficult. Alas, after managing to resist his blandishments, despite her fondness for him, for some time, she eventually had to succumb to them in pure charity: Sir Geoffrey unexpectedly fell seriously in love, but was disappointed in his suit, and where perhaps a man of more innate strength of character would have rallied, Geoffrey fell into a morbid decline, until earlier fears for his stability turned to a very real concern for his reason. So back poor Harriet had to go, her brother's abandoned grief and sick fancies adding years to her, until she began to feel, in fact, more like his mother than his sister, and far, far older than in reality she was. If her friends had not rallied to her, she had no notion how she would have contrived, but gradually the worst crisis was overcome, and the slow return to normality begun. In vain her hopes, however, for a renewal of her freedom: with the improvement of his health and spirits, Geoffrey became ever more demanding and spoiled, his selfish behavior toward many impressionable young women whom he had first charmed causing bitter words, unhappy thoughts, and constant vigilance on the part of his sister to avoid such awkward situations. At one time there was fear of a duel with a brother, at another the threat of a lawsuit, and finally the inevitable blow fell with the near suicide of Selina Markham, one of his foolishly fond little victims.

Unexpectedly, this proved Harriet's salvation: it was too much, she felt at last, her patience, determined spirits, and constant bracing good sense almost exhausted. Already under pressure from her many kind friends to escape from the all-pervading concerns of her brother, she was beginning to agree with them that while she remained to protect, advise, and help him, Geoffrey would never become a responsible being. And while such thoughts ran through her head, Fate intervened for her. For after this affair of Selina Markham's near suicide, although the matter was kept close, it was felt that for the social ease of all those involved, Sir Geoffrey must absent himself for a period of time. Nothing loath, after the first sobering shock, to avoid the discomfort of disapproval, he allowed himself to be persuaded to travel abroad for some months, and as he proposed to spend a good deal of time in Italy, where he had many Italianate friends, Harriet was at last relieved of her burden of responsibility. Briefly, admittedly, Sir Geoffrey attempted to persuade her to accompany him, but having at last made a firm break, she clung tenaciously to her resolution and refused. Observing the direct gaze from the clear brown eyes, and the fastidious delicacy of her mouth, Geoffrey concluded that among his acquaintances in Italy, where manners and behavior were more lax, Harriet might well prove more of an encumbrance than the useful chaperon she had been in England. He therefore forebore to persuade her further.

So at last she was free, unencumbered—and lost. She had literally forgotten how to indulge herself by doing as *she* pleased, and felt a constant sense of guilt whenever, determinedly, she set about attempting to enjoy herself. With looks, comfortable means, intelligence, and charm, for the first time in her life she lacked direction, a sense of purpose. With her usual competence, however, she set about remedying this, deciding that the first necessity was to establish herself independently and comfortably, domestically. She would not continue in her brother's house; and Frome Hall, her husband's seat, had with his death gone by entail to his first cousin, whose kind and cordial invitation to remove to a pleasant house on the estate she had, at the time, refused, finding the surroundings redolent with memories too painful to support. Now, with all of Surrey to choose from, she settled to rent a small gem of a house, set in pleasant grounds, on a gentle slope of the Downs near Dorking. It was reasonably modern and compact, the large bay windows swelling gently each side of the miniature pillared portico, the slender fanlights, and the sparkling white walls, already adorned in places with lacey wisteria, pleasing her aesthetic taste. It was, moreover, within easy distance of several of her dearest friends; and so, with a small staff and a brisk elderly aunt, always a favorite, as companion, she attempted to begin her life anew.

Having thus organized her domestic arrangements, she next turned her attention to other matters. Aware that, if she were not careful, a moneyed, still young woman living alone and independent with only a chaperon for company could easily appear at best an Eccentric, she busied herself, through her friends, with the not inconsiderable social life of the county, and between giving and receiving invitations, and attending to her charitable duties in the parish, she gradually became happy and unexceptionable again, and very much sought after as a guest. For as well as being gay and amusing, she was kind, and although, with the disappearance of that watchful motherliness characteristic of her when Geoffrey was present, she seemed considerably younger, she was yet old enough to be considered "safe" by the very young ladies and their mammas, and by the nervous bachelors of all ages, to be found in every society.

One morning in early spring, then, with her brother's sojourn in Italy happily prolonged by him yet again, she was dressing to pay a visit for a few days to two of her dearest friends, Mr. Edward Keithley and his wife Anne. In view of the closeness of this friendship, her aunt, Miss Marion Neligan, had expressed her desire to stay at home. She had, she said, spent so long in an elder sister's house, where she was never considered anything but a useless guest and a necessary evil, that she could never have enough of the affection, freedom, and feeling of security that always surrounded her at Dorking. Her room, her small duties, her authority with the pleasant servants, which she shared equally with Harriet, delighted her, and she would invariably prefer to remain in such surroundings than visit elsewhere. Harriet had laughingly agreed, and having now finished her toilette, descended the small curved staircase, with its delicately wrought-bronze handrail, ready to leave on her visit to the Keithleys. From below, Miss Neligan surveyed her niece's descent with affectionate approval: the air of elegance and breeding, the set of the small head in its dark green hat with the jaunty curled feather, the discreet drape of the matching traveling dress, its cuffs and collar embroidered *à la militaire*, which yet did not hide Harriet's graceful figure—enchanting! And the smile, at once happy, affectionate, and sincere, bestowed on her aunt— yet again, Miss Neligan felt her sentimental heart swell. She turned to accompany Harriet to the door, and then talking gaily, they went out and down the three curved steps to the gravel sweep, where Harriet's phaeton, the only dashing thing she had allowed herself, stood waiting with the groom holding the heads of the matching bays. Behind this, the light carriage held her boxes, her maid, and the coachman, who had his usual instructions to follow at a reasonable distance. In no time at all, Harriet was up and, with a final wave, away, handling the bays to a nicety, and guiding them fast between the narrow posts of the gate.

She was a skilled whip, fast yet not foolhardy, and within the space of less than an hour, was gently tooling the phaeton up to the main door of Mr. Keithley's imposing residence, which he had but recently inherited. Even as she reined in, and house and stable servants flurried round, a tall fair girl some years younger than Harriet herself ran lightly down the steps, followed by a dark handsome man somewhat older, his rather severe countenance bearing a warm smile of welcome.

"I'm so glad you are come early!" exclaimed Anne Keithley, kissing Harriet with great affection, and glancing round at her husband for his agreement. "I know you said you would *try* to, but something always seems to prevent it!"

Harriet laughed. "Well, today, as you see, I traveled without Marion, and that accounts for it—no forgotten gloves, no last-minute changes of pelisse, no sudden alarms!" She gave her hand to Edward Keithley, who held it in a friendly manner, his dark eyes kind, and they all three turned toward the house, Anne chattering gaily, her reserved manner of earlier years quite gone since her happy marriage.

"I expect you collect my telling you two of our guests would already be arrived? Well, they asked sudden leave to bring someone with them, an unexpected visitor, an old friend of the husband's from the North, whom he has had no word of for years—" She hesitated, and as her husband looked at her quizzically, continued,

"I'd like your opinion of him, this friend! He's very distant, and very assured, and extremely tall, but somehow, without any real resemblance of feature, he reminds me of Edward—"

Here she glanced up with great affection at her husband, who said with amusement, "Apart from the fact that he is younger than I, a good six inches as tall again, resembles me in face and figure not at all, and has a deuced haughty way with him that I deplore, the resemblance is startling!"

As Harriet laughed, Anne was heard to insist swiftly, "No, but there is an *air* about him, of mystery, or unhappiness—I know not what—that reminds me of you!"

"Well, I was certainly extremely overbearing and miserable when you first encountered me, so perhaps, apart from the mystery, there is *some* resemblance after all!"

On this facetious remark, they entered the house, and such intimate personal observations must, of necessity, cease. With great good humor Edward Keithley left Anne to escort Harriet to her usual bedroom, and returned, presumably to his other guests in another part of the house.

CHAPTER II

Alone in her room after a lively conversation with Anne, and with a good half-hour before a proposed nuncheon, Harriet leaned dreamily against the window, filled with a pleasant melancholy. At one time, some years before she came to know Anne, she had fancied herself in love with Edward Keithley. But he had been, she knew, totally unaware of her feelings, and had always behaved toward her as a friend, rallying to her and her brother in times of trouble. Casually, a little sadly, she looked back over her earlier life . . . so much now lost, forgotten . . . her husband dead, and other suitors sacrificed to her sense of responsibility to her brother. . . .Well, there was no reason now for regrets—she was happy as she was, independent, busy, amused, and hoped with all her heart never to become involved emotionally with anyone again. At this point, her pleasant, rather self-satisfied reverie was broken by sounds of activity below in the garden, and looking down, she observed Anne on the terrace with a young, attractive-looking couple, the woman dark, graceful, somewhere in her early twenties, the man fair, with a fresh complexion, nearer her own age. Upon Anne looking up as she looked down, and calling to her to descend and meet Jane and George Bentley, she turned, and pausing only to pick up a light shawl from the drawer where her maid had already placed it, hurried down for her introductions. The Bentleys, she learned, came from Dorset, which accounted for her not knowing them previously. On first acquaintance, they seemed pleasant, unexceptionable, and if the truth were told, a little dull, and she fell to wondering, as she conducted an easy conversation with them, where their haughty and mysterious friend had gone to. Her speculation was satisfied by George Bentley saying that Hugh De Brandon never descended from his room before midday or so, professing himself to have difficulty, if he were so rash as to do so, in getting through the rest of the day. Harriet could not resist remarking dryly that he sounded rather world-weary, and was rewarded with a speaking look from Jane Bentley and a sober observation that he had, perhaps, reason to be at odds with the world. There was an expectant pause, but nothing came of it, and Harriet was left to remark, crossly to herself this time, that the lack of humor of Mrs. Bentley's reply was unredeemed by any clarification of her dark hint of some ill fortune or worse in Hugh De Brandon's life.

Within a very short period of time, however, she found herself accompanying the others to the small salon to partake of a light repast, and feeling intrigued to observe this controversial guest at close quarters. On entering the salon, her curiosity was satisfied, for in the far corner, leaning negligently near the long windows, was a tall dark figure, at first glance willowy, but subsequently with a breadth of shoulder clearly visible against the light from outside. Her immediate impression, from across the room, was fully in support of Edward Keithley's opinion: the thick black hair, arranged in a severe Brutus style, the simple, faultlessly cut coat of dark brown broadcloth, the elegantly discreet cravat, the white breeches and untasseled gleaming hessians, bespoke the austere dandy (an unlovable combination, in Harriet's view). On his coming immediately forward, with some address, to be presented, she therefore put out her hand distantly, observing him coolly with no hint of her usual smile. It was with something of a shock she remarked the mocking expression in the handsome dark gray eyes. The face was long and tapering, the forehead broad under heavily marked straight brows, the mouth long, too, yet full, the jawline strong and narrow. The cynical amusement in the eyes was repeated in the amused curl of the mouth, the whole dark countenance seeming redolent of experience, cynicism, and contempt, but whether for women or the world at large she could not guess. Holding her hand in a firm, yet detached fashion, he said surprisingly, in deep, languid tones, "So this is Sir Geoffrey's sister."

Temporarily off balance, she looked swiftly for explanation to Anne, only to catch an expression of complete bewilderment on her friend's face. Giving herself a mental shake, therefore, for she had been long enough in the world to acquire considerable poise and a distinct dislike of being deliberately scored off, she replied sweetly, a cold gleam in her eye that belied the demure manner of her observation, "And *you* are a friend of Geoffrey's!

Indeed, one never ceases to be amazed at the number and variety of his acquaintances!"

An even more amused flicker of the eye showed her point well taken, and appreciated, but his answer was wholly deplorable, for he said, with studied calm, "But you are far, far different from how I had imagined you, Lady Frome. From Geoffrey's description, I had thought you somewhat older and far, far fiercer—almost the doyen, in fact, of his world . . . I must take him severely to task when next I see him."

Harriet experienced a sudden contraction of her heart. She knew Geoffrey made use of her, yet afterward often perversely resented her subsequent unavoidable intervention in his affairs; but somehow she had persuaded herself that in his heart he appreciated her help, was very fond of her, and would never, in any circumstances, belittle or criticize her, deliberately and disloyally, to his friends. Now that faith was destroyed, and for an unguarded moment, her face must have revealed her hurt. Realizing this too late, she looked up into the mocking gray eyes above her with all expression wiped from her face to smile coldly, and turn away in a manner that left no misunderstanding of her censure of his behavior. But as she glanced up, some shadow, some nuance of feeling—was it shame, sympathy?—showed momentarily in his expression. It was gone in an instant, the moment passed, and both with tacit dislike separated to talk with others of their friends.

Fortunately, this exchange was noted by no one else, as Anne, immediately after her introduction, had turned away to speak again with Jane Bentley, and Edward Keithley entering the room at that very moment, his attention was taken up with George Bentley. Harriet could not but be grateful for this: in the present company, nothing good could come of the knowledge that Mr. De Brandon had deliberately flaunted Geoffrey's cruel disloyalty to his sister. None knew better than Anne Keithley, who had been Selina's sister, Anne Markham, before her marriage to Edward, how Harriet had suffered, the strain she had been under in attempting to control her brother's reprehensible behavior during the entire affair of Selina Markham's attempted suicide, or the deep distress she had felt that Geoffrey could behave in so reprehensible a fashion. And now her sisterly affection was mocked by a stranger, a friend of Sir Geoffrey's. Indeed, had Anne been a party to the exchange, she would have been herself overset for her friend's sake, and Harriet considered grimly that the mysterious visitor was fortunate in that Edward Keithley, too, was unaware of his uninvited guest's behavior.

Harriet was made of sterner stuff, however, and soon forced herself to forget both the incident and her hurt, at least until she should be alone and could indulge her feelings. She had no wish to know *where* her brother and his unpleasant friend had met, but judging by the hard manner and cynical demeanor of the newcomer, she suspicioned it was somewhere among that society for which she had no use. That she was right in this assumption, and that he had met Geoffrey among his libertine friends in Rome, was obvious after some conversation during the nuncheon, Hugh De Brandon comparing his host's luscious hothouse grapes favorably with those in Tuscany, a region he knew, he said, almost as well as he knew Rome and its environs, and asking, with seemingly real interest, to be shown the vine, now well-nigh one hundred and fifty years old, from which they came. She could not help but observe that, despite Edward Keithley's earlier criticism of him, the two men had much to say to each other, and, as both had an indefinable air of surprise and satisfaction with each other, judged this to be the first occasion they had had an opportunity to meet and converse for any length of time. Indeed, that Edward Keithley had at least to some extent revised his earlier opinion of the visitor was obvious when, as the party broke up after their meal, he invited Hugh De Brandon, without any necessity to be so civil, to ride round the home park with him after the proposed visit to the vine. George Bentley was kindly invited to do so as an afterthought, but declined, saying with a laugh that he preferred feminine company, if they would have him. So the party broke up, and Harriet, though she would have dearly loved to be alone, to compose her mind and rest, a nervous headache threatening to cause her some distress, felt she must, out of courtesy, remain with Anne and the Bentleys.

They wandered out onto the sheltered terrace again with only their shawls for outer protection, the early March sunshine being unexpectedly warm there, and, sitting on the stone seats, over which the servants had strewn gay cushions, made desultory conversation. Soon, however, Jane Bentley, whom Harriet had begun to judge as pretty, empty-headed, a little overconsequential, and a born gossip of what might be termed the "innuendo" school, began to indulge this hobby; she said, with an arch look at Harriet, "And how do you find Hugh De Brandon, Lady Frome?"

If she had not been certain of Jane's attentions being elsewhere during her own earlier unpleasant interlude with Mr. De Brandon, Harriet might have thought Mrs. Bentley to have been aware of it, but as things were, she had no such fears. So, feeling a little for George Bentley, whose confused expression revealed his opinion that his wife's query lacked delicacy, she replied composedly, "Indeed, I hardly had time to form any opinion; he is indeed tall, is he not?"

Anne's lips quivered, George looked as if he considered his wife to have received a mild set-down, and Jane Bentley, sensing in her foolish mind some slight disapproval, bridled a little, determined to impress.

"He is a very strange man! George had not seen him since his Oxford days, you know, knew nothing of him until, quite by chance, he arrived at our house at Manford Parva a week ago. He had been traveling across the country from some friend in Devon, on his way to London, when one of his horses cast a shoe, or a trace broke, or some such small disaster, causing his carriage to lodge fast in a ditch, from which it could not be raised until morning. And the village inn affording but little in the way of comfort, he recollected George's living in the vicinity, and leaving his servant to attend to one horse at the hostelry as best he could, rode the other the short distance to our house."

George was heard to remark that it was fortunate he had not called two days earlier, or he would have found them from home, on a visit to his sister in the south of the county. But this mild attempt at a diversion had no effect of restraining his wife. Barely allowing him time to finish his observation, she continued.

"It was most annoying—I began to feel quite deserted! They had once been kindred spirits, you know, and so George and Hugh were ever talking, in the library, or riding together about the estate, or some such thing. Anyway, one confidence led to another, and so far as we could later put the matter together, it seems that"—(here she lowered her voice, and despite an inarticulate strangled objection from her husband, continued—"he had had a very unhappy and unsatisfactory marriage, and his wife had killed herself because of his cruelty to her!"

In the shocked silence that followed, everyone being appalled not only by the story, but by the crass mind which could divulge it to comparative strangers, George said loudly, angrily, and with a heightened color, "Jane, be quiet! You have no business to talk so! Part of this is conjecture, and anyway, whatever Hugh said to me was in confidence ... I beg you will excuse us, Mrs. Keithley, Lady Frome."

He bowed stiffly, took his wife's arm in an ungentle manner, and almost marched her off, his back rigid with disapproval, undoubtedly to give her a thorough set-down in private. Harriet felt a little sorry for him, yet could not but censure him for obviously divulging his friend's confidences, and discussing them, with a woman whom he must know to be at best an indiscreet rattle.

Left alone, Anne and Harriet, after one swift glance at each other, remained silent, both busy with their thoughts. It occurred to Harriet that, with the image of Hugh De Brandon vivid in their minds, Anne, having overheard him in the salon claiming acquaintance with Geoffrey, must be wondering how they had met, but the delicacy of her mind prevented her from questioning what Harriet herself had not volunteered. She remarked, therefore, in a casual voice, looking at Anne's reflective profile, "I collect you were as astonished as I to hear Mr. De Brandon claim acquaintanceship with Geoffrey this morning?"

Anne looked up swiftly, a little apprehensively.

"Indeed, it came as a shock ... he ... I had hoped

..." she went on in a rush, "that is, he does not seem such a man as I should like your brother to associate with if Geoffrey is, as we hope, attempting to become a little—steadier—in his ways! But perhaps," she added hopefully, "the acquaintance is not a recent one, and belongs to Geoffrey's wilder days."

Reflecting cynically on Anne's gentle nature, which always determinedly looked for the best in everyone, and probably believed in Geoffrey's promised reform, Harriet said dryly, "Indeed, I fear not! I suspicion they have been recently together in Italy, since during nuncheon Mr. De Brandon mentioned being lately in Italy, and earlier deliberately informed me that Geoffrey had spoken of me to him. In no pleasant fashion, I was given to understand." She looked up, able, with so close, kind, and sensitive a friend as Anne, and one with whom she had shared so much earlier adversity, to reveal some of her distress. And Anne, full of sympathy, put her hand over the elder woman's, saying softly, "Geoffrey does not mean it, you know. He was forever striking poses, taking color from whomever he was with at the time, and saying what he thought would best amuse and appeal to them."

This tacit analysis, and oblique disapproval, of Mr. De Brandon's character was so akin to her own opinion that Harriet had to laugh, and her somber mood vanished. Rising gracefully to her feet, she said briskly, "Come, you always like to walk. Let us dress more warmly and take a turn up to the knoll, and tell each other all the news of the past two weeks."

And so they set off on their quite considerable walk, in perfect amity, their very different styles of beauty complementing each other, the watery sunshine casting a halo around them.

Arrived at the knoll after walking for a quite considerable time, however, they found their companionable solitude broken in that someone was there before them: seated on one of the rustic benches which Mr. Keithley had caused to be placed there were Edward himself and Hugh De Brandon, their mounts tethered some little distance away. Harriet was conscious of a sharp feeling of annoyance and disappointment. Had they approached from the other side, they might have had a glimpse of the two men before being themselves seen, and Harriet felt she might in that case have prevailed on Anne, in her present state of mind, to come quietly away again without disturbing the two men. Now, however, such a course was impossible; they had been seen, the gentlemen were already rising to greet them, and normal courtesy dictated their presence. Accepting the inevitable, Harriet seated herself next to Anne on one of the benches and a desultory conversation followed concerning the glorious view below them, last year's harvest, and the spring blossoms already glimpsed on the trees in the valley. Within a little while, however, Anne was deep in a discussion with her husband about the untidiness of a certain tenant's garden, and would have him walk a little down, and to one side of, the knoll where the offending family's ground could be observed. Harriet thus found herself alone, and uncomfortable, with Mr. De Brandon. Added to her justifiable resentment of his previous rudeness, she had the knowledge that, admittedly through no fault of hers, she was aware of a distressing and intimate side of his own private life. She remained, therefore, looking composedly at the surrounding countryside, but making no attempt to converse with him. Suddenly, however, where she had supposed him to have been, like herself, gazing out over the valley, she realized that he had in fact been regarding her profile, and this with some concentration. Her color rose, and angry with herself, she turned to look directly at him. At once his eyes dropped, covering whatever expression had been in them, and he said in a low voice, with none of his customary drawl, "Lady Frome, I owe you an apology. I can make no excuses for my behavior, but only beg you to forgive me my boorishness when I spoke to you of your brother this morning."

Surprised at his change of manner, and even more of heart, Harriet could for the moment say nothing, and he continued, the old, mocking note creeping back into his voice, but with himself the butt this time. "It may be hardly credible, but I am not always so—so *gauche*. Indeed, I have the reputation of being, at times, quite a pleasant fellow. But temperamental, alas. Increasingly so these last few years."

Thinking the handsomeness of his apology a little tarnished by the casual plea of being subject to whims, and reflecting that *that* was no reason, or excuse, for rude and hurtful behavior, Harriet nevertheless smiled, and begged him, conventionally, to speak no more of the incident, saying she had forgot it already.

"No," he said in a low voice, once again without any hint of mockery, "that you have not; and I can hardly blame you. Would it improve matters if I told you that Geoffrey was not so brutally direct in his criticism as I gave you to understand, and that I may therefore have mistaken him?"

Harriet's sense of humor got the better of her, and laughing, she said, "No, that it would *not*! Now I *know* what you told me of Geoffrey's opinion is correct, for he was always devious in his criticisms, and never directly censorious in his life!"

For an instant, he studied her face seriously, then accepting her reply, laughed, in his turn, in relief. And Anne, returning at this moment with her husband, had the surprise of seeing her dearest friend on apparently amicable terms with a man whom, but a short while earlier, they had both professed to dislike and distrust.

CHAPTER III

Harriet's visit was to have lasted a fortnight, but in the event a series of misadventures eventually considerably shortened it. The first of these occurred some five days or so after her arrival. The guests had been augmented by another young couple, and also by Selina, Anne's younger sister, who had returned from a prolonged visit to friends in the North of England to stay with her sister and brother-in-law. Harriet had, of course, seen her periodically since her attempted suicide, but never for any length of time, Anne and Edward wishing to avoid pain and embarrassment between Sir Geoffrey's sister and one of his foolishly affectionate inamoratas. Now, on renewed acquaintance, Harriet had found Selina much improved: she would always be silly, light in her affections, easily influenced, and without discernment, but she was never now sulky, or resentful. Appreciating her sister's concern to make her happy, and enjoying consequently a very full life, her radiant looks quite restored, she had become a reasonably pleasant, normal young woman, and at this moment looking forward with great delight to a renewed stay with Anne and Edward, and particularly to the ball that her brother-in-law was to give that evening. There had been bustle all day in preparation for this function: one little maid had had near hysterics on dropping a very valuable vase, the second footman had wrenched his ankle hanging garlands from the gallery by means of a ladder, the cook was bothering the housekeeper with ambitious revisions for one of the desserts, and Anne and Edward had begun to think themselves insane for embarking on a ball but a short while before the London Season began.

However, at the eleventh hour all was well, and some little time before the guests were due to arrive, the house party assembled in the large drawing room. Selina was radiant in soft pink, with her fair curls caught up to one side in a nosegay of tiny flowers; Anne slight, delicate, like an ice-maiden in pale, shimmering green satin; and the other two young women graceful, one in celestial blue crepe open over pale ivory satin, the other in yellow silk. But it was Harriet, vital, beautiful, in a bronze gown shaped more to her waist, in the latest fashion, her mother's sapphires sparkling on her slender neck, her heavy brown-gold hair dressed high and caught with a sapphire spray, who drew all eyes, quenching Selina's doll-like prettiness and dimming even Anne's ethereal beauty. Unaware of the impression she had created, for she was not vain, she felt rather than saw Hugh De Brandon's bold, speculative stare, and experienced a sudden

uncharacteristic embarrassment as though, with his un-
doubted and questionable experience, he was aware of everything about her, from her thoughts to the tingling in
her feet in anticipation of the dancing she so loved. But
there was little time for such reflections, since very shortly
the first carriages rolled up the drive and the county began to arrive.

From the start, the ball was a great success, everyone
being fond of the Keithleys and determined to enjoy their
hospitality. Harriet found herself in great demand, but
having been intrigued as well as unnerved by Hugh De
Brandon's scrutiny, she now found herself disappointed in
his subsequent apparent indifference to her. Angry at herself, she yet could not avoid glancing from time to time,
from among the group surrounding her, or in the middle
of a set, or awaiting the arrival of a glass of ratafia from
some helpful escort, for a glimpse of the tall elegant figure. But in vain; after making himself agreeable generally,
and dancing a supposedly "duty" set with his hostess,
Hugh De Brandon retired to the card room, and was seen
no more by the dancers. There had, indeed, been one moment when Harriet had thought he intended to approach
her, but to her chagrin another neighbor of Edward
Keithley's, Sir Henry Bohun, a pleasant, well-set-up man
of about her own age whom she later learned to be still a
bachelor and a great "catch," was at that moment introduced to her, and obviously attracted to her, he at once
monopolized her, so that when eventually she was able to
free herself, she found Mr. De Brandon to have wandered
off elsewhere. But it was of no use to repine; indeed,
when she considered her interest in Hugh De Brandon's
whereabouts, she was astonished at herself, since she was
never easy with him, had but recently disliked him in-

tensely, and even now had little time for his frequently languid, disinterested airs. Deciding that the only reason for her desire for his presence was to show her indifference to him, she eventually dismissed him completely from her mind, and gave herself wholeheartedly, this time, to her enjoyment.

It chanced that, part way through the evening, some unskillful young gentleman, anxious to carry a syllabub to his partner, spilled it instead on the hem of Harriet's gown. Cutting short, in the kindest manner possible, his anguished apologies (for he somehow reminded her of Geoffrey before time and circumstances had spoiled him), she withdrew to her room in order to sponge some of the stickiness away. Her chamber looked over the front carriage drive, and she had just completed her task without calling her abigail, when she was disturbed to hear the sound of galloping hooves approaching the main door. Something in the urgency of their arrival, at a hard gallop, presaged disaster, and when the heavy bell jangled forcibly, she was already down the quiet corridor and descending the staircase even at the same time as the butler, a disapproving expression on his face, walked along the hall to open the door. She was therefore a close spectator of the scene which followed, indeed at this stage the only one, for the gay music in the ballroom where a country dance was in progress, and the ebb and flow of chatter from supper and reception rooms, prevented any sound of the urgent bell being heard on that floor except in the Servants' Hall.

On entering, the new arrival appeared as dramatic as his approach to the house had been: spattered in mud, his riding coat dripping moisture, his face drawn with fatigue, he leaned heavily on the lintel of the door and asked hoarsely for Mr. De Brandon. The butler, obviously impressed by what he saw, and therefore ignoring the fact that the messenger was no gentleman but a groom and thus should have made his presence known at another, less imposing, entrance, waved his hand imperiously toward one of the heavy oak chairs set against the wall near the door, and summoning the footman now hovering behind him, sent him to the reception rooms in search of Mr. De Brandon. He himself turned toward the ballroom, and Harriet, instinctively helpful, said she would visit the card room. After his initial surprise at seeing her on the stairs behind him, the butler thanked her with relief, and set off toward the crush to find Hugh De Brandon.

Harriet saw him even as she entered the small card room: he was leaning back, an expression of indifference on his face, one long brown muscular hand holding his cards, the other dangling casually over the back of his chair. At her appearance in the doorway, he looked up, and seeing something of stress in her countenance, rose immediately, his cards still in his hand, to approach her. Regarding the worried frown steadily, he said at once, "Is there anything amiss? Can I help in any way?"

Eager only that he should receive whatever news the rider had for him at once, she replied, without preamble, "There is a messenger in the hall who would seem to have ridden feverishly with some news for you"—and then, seeing the sudden apprehension in his expression, added with great concern—"I hope indeed it is nothing serious . . . shall I find Edward for you, in case you should wish to speak with him?"

His look dark, troubled, and somehow stormy, he paused only to thank her, then with a hurried apology to the others at the card table, turned on his heel and left.

Finding Edward unobtrusively might have taken some little while, but she was fortunate in discovering him as he was making his way from the ballroom to ascertain that his less active guests were also enjoying themselves. She explained the circumstances rapidly therefore, and at Edward's request, since Anne was nowhere to be seen, returned with him to the hall. Hugh De Brandon had just dismissed the groom, and looking extremely grave came up to them, saying, "Mr. Keithley, I must ask you to forgive me—but I must be packed and leave at once. I have passed a very pleasant few days here, and I thank you for your hospitality, but"—here he hesitated, and then continued jerkily, low, and with none of his usual ease of manner—"My daughter, she is but eight years old . . . my wife is dead, you know . . . has from time to time a kind of, of *crise de nerfs*—a hysteria—that affects her physically, so that she sometimes even loses the use of her limbs."

Here, as he paused, he caught Harriet's look of pity and concern, and addressing himself rather to her, went on. "It is since her mother's death. I have had physicians, specialists . . . but although they are all agreed that the affliction may be to a great extent mental rather than physical in its origin, not one of them can find a remedy."

He pulled himself up, obviously aware of revealing too much of his carefully guarded, innermost anxieties, and adding only, "I am told she has but now had another serious attack, and her governess has always instructions to send for me when any such symptoms occur," bowed to his listeners, and taking the stairs two at a time with his long legs, disappeared from sight. Edward Keithley at once sent a message to the stables; Harriet attended to telling the housekeeper to have refreshment provided for the but recently arrived groom; Hugh De Brandon's own servant was summoned; and within no time at all, with no ripple on the happy progress of the ball, Hugh De Brandon had left.

Nothing was said of the incident until late the following morning, when, the house guests having eventually all assembled, Hugh De Brandon's absence was of course remarked. On Mr. Keithley's explaining very briefly what had occurred, George Bentley said soberly, "He had a long journey, then, almost to the boundaries of Lancashire ... he should be arrived by this afternoon, however, if, as I suppose, he rode right through the night."

His wife, obviously still subdued after her husband's disapproval the previous day, kept silence, and beyond Mr. Bentley's adding briefly that unhappily he understood Hugh to have great problems with the child, nothing more was said of the matter.

As always happens when something unexpected and uncomfortable occurs, the party was a little subdued for the rest of the day, despite talk of the success of the ball, and little incidents that occurred during it; and when Jane Bentley retired before dinner, which was taken early, with a nervous sick headache, the group felt even further depleted than in fact they were. Next day, his wife fearing the onset of one of her occasional blinding migraines, and anxious to reach her own bed, in her own home, before this set in, George Bentley, too, said an apologetic farewell to his host, and left early in the forenoon, Jane Bentley leaning wearily back against the cushioned seats of their well-sprung carriage, her maid, her vinaigrette, and numerous shawls disposed around her, and George himself riding alongside.

The house party now being reduced to the other young couple, Selina, Harriet, and Edward Keithley and Anne themselves, all pleasantly disposed toward one another, matters began to pick up, but the following day things were again thrown awry by Harriet receiving a message from her own housekeeper that her aunt was suffering from a putrid sore throat, the doctor had been called, and adding that although Miss Neligan herself was loud in her instructions that Harriet not be told, the housekeeper felt otherwise, as Miss Harriet well knew her aunt to be a bad invalid, always anxious to be up and about again too soon. Harriet could not but concur in this criticism, and understand her housekeeper's unwillingness to take charge of such a situation; besides, she was concerned for her aunt herself, who though remarkably healthy and resilient, was yet an elderly lady. Accordingly, she felt she, too, must leave, and regretfully saying farewell to her friends, and hoping for a reunion, preferably at Dorking this time, in the near future, drove off in her phaeton, the other carriage following behind, the way she had come.

On arrival home, Harriet went directly to her aunt's room, the housekeeper having met her with a grave face, as she descended from the phaeton, to tell her that Miss Neligan seemed not much improved. Regarding the elderly lady as she sat, birdlike, up in bed, her rather sparse gray hair in a neat topknot and covered by a jaunty beribboned cap, her bed gown and dressing jacket pristine fresh, the bed itself neat as a new pin, Harriet felt matters to be by no means as desperate as the housekeeper had led her to believe, and that she had no cause for alarm. That the invalid had an exceedingly harsh cough, however, and a bad congestion of the lungs, could not be denied, and Harriet was relieved to be at home to take charge of her aunt's recovery, which proved unexpectedly slow, partly because, in the doctor's opinion, Miss Neligan would never relax, but must always be talking to her niece, or those few close friends who were permitted to visit her, or netting a purse, or slipping out of bed without her robe to poke unnecessarily at the glowing fire, which a maid could easily have attended to, and indeed did.

Still, by dint of determined overseeing, and cajolery (which her aunt loved to receive), Harriet had Miss Neligan first up and about in her bedchamber, then downstairs during the afternoons, and finally walking for a brief spell in the remarkably warm early spring sunshine in a sheltered corner of the walled garden. To achieve this happy state of affairs had taken three weeks, however, with Harriet so busily occupied that there was no possibility of the Keithleys returning her visit; and now, she knew, they were about to leave for London with Selina. Normally, they would undoubtedly have put off their arrival in the metropolis, and stayed first some little while with Harriet. But this was Selina's first real Season since her misadventure, and they were anxious she should attend it at the earliest opportunity, and enjoy it to the full. Matters seemed at a standstill, therefore, with no chance of a meeting, until Anne had the idea of Harriet and her aunt joining them in London. The Keithleys' townhouse was airy and salubrious, being set overlooking the Park, and while Miss Neligan would have much to amuse her, even in gazing from her window at the busy scene below, Harriet herself would be less confined, while still able to study the progress of the now near-recovered invalid. On this proposal being put to her by Edward Keithley, who had ridden over especially to do so, Harriet had at first demurred, saying that despite the fresh air in her friends' quarter of London, it could not compare with that of the real countryside, and she felt her aunt would benefit more, and complete her recovery faster, if they remained where they were, in Dorking.

But Miss Neligan, hearing of this, said roundly that it was ridiculous to mope at home, and that Harriet was not, ever again, to put herself out for lame ducks.

"I should have thought you would have had enough of self-sacrifice," she said crossly. "Why, you have only just escaped from that selfish young brother of yours, and now you must go making a martyr of yourself for me! I know how much you would enjoy a sojourn in Town"—which was true enough—"and it won't be I who prevents it!"

Looking at the mixed emotions which chased over Harriet's face, she continued, with a twinkle. "Besides, truth to tell, I myself would *vastly* prefer London! I have not visited there for many years, not since I was a young girl, in fact, and although it must be very much changed, I cannot but think that it will be for the better!"

"But your health," began Harriet, who could not help smiling at her aunt's youthful enthusiasm.

"Stuff and nonsense, girl! You don't want for sense— you must realize that, at my time of life, my health improves by doing what I *want* to do, not what my physician tells me!"

And so, since nothing could move Miss Neligan from this opinion, and since, moreover, she had the willing co-operation of the Keithleys, it was arranged that, allowing a few days for further recovery on the one side, and for settling in on the other, Harriet and Miss Neligan should join Anne, Edward, and Selina in Park Lane within a sennight.

CHAPTER IV

Harriet stretched luxuriously, wriggled her toes under the bedcovers, and gazed sideways, beyond the top of the tester bed, at the pale green ceiling with its ornate boss and frieze of dancing nymphs. It was wonderful to be in London again ... she had forgot the excitement, the endless bustle, the gowns, the spectacles, the routs, soirées, and grand balls. Even the morning calls or visits with her aunt to the Circulating Library, or with Selina, perhaps, to the milliner's, were full of amusement and interest. She was surprised and delighted that former acquaintances remembered her, and welcomed her back into their circle with warmth, and that new friends, too, appeared to find her agreeable company.

Already she had been in London for nigh on a fortnight, and during that time she had danced and talked, and visited the play to her heart's content; had even had the rare delight of accompanying Anne and Edward to hear Lucia Vestris sing. Her aunt, too, had proved her point about happiness and inclination being great healers, being now in far more robust health. Although naturally not eager to join in the energetic pleasures of a Society far younger than herself, Marion Neligan was delighted to take her place among the dowagers and watch the colorful world go past before her eyes; and in this manner she often acted as chaperon to Selina, who had developed a strangely strong affection for her—this, Harriet privately opined, because the brisk, elderly lady, with her unflagging interest in other people and her determined optimism, was so vastly different from the ailing, disappointed, querulous woman Selina had known in her mother. Miss Neligan's interests, too, while differing in being tempered by strong common sense, were just as fresh and ingenuous as Selina's, and a strong bond of friendship was thus forged, which all felt to be an excellent influence on Selina's character.

Everything, in fact, was set fair, and there could hardly have been a more equable, contented household in all fashionable London. But idylls seldom last intact for long: the first small cloud appeared on Harriet's horizon on the evening of the very day when she had lain so contentedly, dreaming idly in bed. She was at a rout party given by Sir Henry Bohun, that bachelor who had first met her at Mr. Keithley's ball, now some time past, and who, on her arrival in Town, had eagerly renewed his acquaintance with her, meeting her in the Row, or calling on the Keithleys as a friend, much to Anne and Edward's amusement. This evening, therefore, as far as his duties as an excellent host permitted, he was inevitably her close companion at his own rout, and privately Harriet, while reasonably safe from gossip by having a number of admirers present, was yet beginning to feel a little hedged in by his constant attentions. The rout, too, she felt to be a crush, and she began to be a prey to fatigue, an unusual state of affairs for her. She moved therefore, as soon as she conveniently could, to sit quietly on an elegant striped settee which, being half hidden by heavy brocade curtains in a bay of the drawing room, had remained unnoticed by others seeking somewhere to rest for a while. Alone, at ease, and so fast recovering her energy and spirits, she gradually became aware of the noisy conversation of two very young men, both what her brother would have called a little foxed, taking place just beyond the curtain. They were discussing the recent visit one of them had made to Rome, and the ways of the Anglo-Italian Society there. From their endless anecdotes and observations, interspersed with loud laughter, she deduced those ways to be often dissolute, and with Geoffrey immediately in the forefront of her mind, while attempting to avoid eavesdropping, could not help but overhear some of the more disturbing snatches of dialogue. When her brother's name actually occurred, she dropped all attempt to struggle with her notions of good breeding and listened anxiously. He was described as amusing, a great favorite, but ever in some one or other ridiculous amorous situation. The latest *on-dit*, it seemed, was of a torrid affair with a Countess D'Antiglione, whose complacent, elderly husband was at last aroused, and like to cause a scandal.

Alarmed, Harriet yet knew that there was nothing she could do; she knew, too, that Geoffrey would almost certainly, with his usual facile charm, adeptly extricate himself at the last minute. But next morning she found her wholehearted enjoyment of the London scene lessened, her anxiety assailing her at odd moments, whatever her occupation or amusement at the time. During the next few days she rallied determinedly, however, and once again attempted to exercise her natural resilience and strong common sense to ignore the matter, since she was powerless to alter it. But it was difficult, and the presence of Selina, Anne, and Edward, who had all been concerned in Geoffrey's worst escapade, did not help matters. Indeed, she was regarding Selina soberly one morning, thinking again of past worries and fears, when the girl looked up, and with a sudden smile that much enhanced her prettiness, came to sit beside Harriet, saying with a self-conscious little laugh, "You were regarding me as you had used to—with apprehension!"

And then, as Harriet, conscience-stricken, made haste to demur, continued. "But you must not, you know. Mr. Huntley, who is so frequently here, has done me the honor of asking if he may pay his addresses to me, and is but now hopefully speaking to Mr. Keithley."

Harriet was delighted: she had observed Mr. Huntley, a pleasant young man of some twenty-three years, constantly dancing attendance on Selina, and had hoped something might come of it. Moreover, concerned as she had but now been in remembering past anxieties, she was even more pleased to hear Selina add, a little shyly, "And I—I should like you to know that I have forgot Sir Geoffrey utterly; indeed, he was far too old for me, above all else, and I should, I know, have been miserable even had his intentions been sincere."

Reeling a little at suddenly finding her brother relegated, as it were, to at best a middle-aged trifler, Harriet's sense of humor almost overcame her, but knowing how ungracious, even hurtful, such a reaction would be, and how demoralizing to her young companion, she hid all trace of her amusement, saying only, with great gentleness, "I am so *very* glad for you, Selina, and I hope Mr. Keithley, as your guardian, will favor Mr. Huntley's suit."

Selina accepted this speech complacently, and with such happiness that Harriet was indeed touched. The sequel was even more satisfactory from the point of view of one who was still concerned, despite the improvement in her character and spirits, for Selina's future. For after remaining together companionably for some little time, Selina, leaving Harriet seated at the window, was about to run up to her bedchamber to fetch some embroidery which she had rather unwillingly embarked on, when the young lover in question entered the room. Ignoring, or perhaps not observing Harriet, he walked hastily across to Selina, and taking her hand said, in triumphant tones, "Well, *that* is settled! We may become affianced at once, and although your guardian says we must wait a year to be married, why that is not so long after all, for we may see a great deal of each other ... and," he added with gentleness, "you will by then, he feels, have *quite* recovered from your earlier misfortunes."

But at this speech Selina's head went up, and the old, familiar stormy expression, the trembling lip, the swift flush of anger, were, regrettably, to be seen once more. Harriet, anxious only to get up and leave the lovers to themselves, felt suddenly that by drawing attention to her presence she might do more harm than good, and had perforce to remain where she was.

"A whole *year*! No! I won't! I *will not* have my—

my—Mr. Keithley interfering again in my affairs! It is too much—"

"That's enough, Sel," said Mr. Huntley in firm tones, drawing an astonished gaze from his inamorata, and stopping her protestations in midflight.

"But, I—"

"I said *enough*, my dear, so don't enact me a Cheltenham tragedy! We're fortunate to have secured the agreement of *both* parties because, you know, with all due respect, I had the devil of a job to convince m'father it was *you* I wanted to marry—apart from your guardian being a bit of a stickler over everything, too. So don't fly up in the boughs—because it's no use, and it *ain't comfortable*!"

At this masterful speech, the petulant mouth dropped open to a round "O" with astonishment. There was an ominous pause, while Harriet trembled and tried to appear to find the view of the tall houses at the corner, with their ordinary, polished bronze doorknockers, and the view of the Park opposite, utterly fascinating. But, after a horrified moment, Selina appeared to decide that *this* was what a romantic young woman required, a masterful, competent husband who knew what he was about. And although, to Harriet's eyes, the sight of the sturdy young man, with his springy red hair and fierce blue gaze, could hardly be deemed so, it was obvious that Selina thought him the epitome of all that was romantic and manly.

Feeling this to be an opportune moment, Harriet therefore hastened forward to offer her very real congratulations, and adroitly left the sensible young man to enjoy a few brief moments alone with Selina.

With a considerably lightened heart, for it is always pleasurable to find matters falling out happily for those we love and are concerned for, she climbed the staircase to her bedchamber, and collecting her primrose velvet pelisse from the closet, walked over to the cheval mirror to adjust her gown before putting on her high-crowned bonnet. The mirror was set at an angle, and reflected another view of the Park, with riders and carriages turning before they wheeled out of vision. Suddenly, she glimpsed a tall figure, riding a beautiful high-stepping black bay, its thick flowing mane, strong, arched neck, and air of nervous power showing it to be a thoroughbred as mettlesome as it was handsome. Something familiar in the set of the rider's shoulders, perhaps, caught her interest, and unlatching the long narrow window she walked out onto the small balcony, with its delicate lacelike iron rails and overhanging canopy, to better observe the rider. With mixed feelings she realized she had not been mistaken: the horseman, now some distance away, and totally unaware of her presence, was Mr. De Brandon. Harriet turned slowly back into the room, carefully fastened the window again, and mechanically continued putting on her outer garments. Then she arranged her mass of soft brown hair smoothly beneath the elegant pale primrose bonnet, and putting on her tan gloves, went to seek Anne, to drive a little in the Park with her, as they had arranged earlier that morning.

Anne did not share Harriet's passion for high-perch phaetons; indeed, apart from not trusting herself in one, she felt them to be not quite the thing for any young matron to be seen in. So it was the brougham, in the capable hands of the second coachman, that presently took them, in the watery spring sunshine, along the fashionable rides of the Park. Inevitably, of course, half to Harriet's chagrin, half to her pleasure, they encountered Mr. De

Brandon returning in the opposite direction, and on his reining in at once, and removing his handsome, curly-brimmed beaver, they stopped to exchange civilities and news. This social progress had never, since her earliest debutante days, ceased to amuse Harriet: for all the distance one covered, one might as well be afoot, since every few yards or so one stopped to greet one's friends and acquaintances, and examine with a discreet eye their fashionable wardrobes while knowing that, in turn, one was under similar scrutiny. Indeed, this was perhaps the only aspect of London that Harriet felt to be a little tedious: one met one's friends constantly, morning and evening anyway, and a good, exhilarating gallop across the Park would have been far preferable. Still, knowing this to be utterly impossible (she sometimes indulged in picturing the chaos that would ensue, the minor disasters, vapors, panic, and recriminations, should she ride so), she made the best of things, and being of a sociable nature and keen wit, found the slow progress not too galling.

Mr. De Brandon, it seemed, had arrived in Town but yesterday, and on Harriet's inquiring, in some trepidation, about his little daughter, explained her to have been the reason for his late arrival. She was recovered physically, and reasonably stable emotionally, it seemed, after her last attack, which had been severe; but she would still talk but little with anyone, and never exhibited those normal childish tendencies to laugh, or play, or run, or even sulk that are the very essence of childhood. On the contrary, she was ever self-contained, withdrawn, and timid, and no one, not even her governess, who was her kind and constant companion, could get close to her.

Suddenly realizing that he had, once again, been led to

talk of his private affairs by reason of the two gentle, concerned, and sensitive faces upturned to his, he broke off abruptly and changed the subject by saying he would perhaps see them at the Hartleys' crush that night since, if he collected aright, Edward Keithley was a close friend of Captain Hartley from their distant days with the Peninsular Army. And on Anne and Harriet's admitting to attending that party that evening, and another two young friends of Anne's approaching in their carriage but that instant, Hugh De Brandon left them and rode off.

During their slow progress back to the house, and later, seated at her escritoire attending to her correspondence, try as she would, Harriet could not dismiss the vision of a small waiflike figure from her mind. Naturally warmhearted, she wondered how the child occupied her days, without mother, brothers, or sisters, or even, Harriet inferred, friends of her own age. That Hugh De Brandon spent some time with his daughter, and was concerned for her, at least sufficiently so to remain with her when she was sick, there could be no doubt. But when she was, as far as possible, healthy, what then? With his talk of Italy, his visits to friends, his attendance in London, his general air and reputation, she doubted if he paid much attention to his daughter *then*. Realizing she did not even know where, or how, he lived, except that he had an estate, according to George Bentley, "somewhere near the boundaries of Lancashire," she fell casually into imagining his background for him, and as this turned out to be distinctly Gothic—gray, gloomy walls, indifferent servants (with their master being much away), and a dumpy middle-aged governess, kind certainly, but with neither real understanding nor any liveliness of spirit, she began to laugh at herself as a second Mrs. Radcliffe. All the same, she was sufficiently intrigued to know more of the mysterious Mr. De Brandon, as well as concerned for his daughter, to dress at her most elegant for the Hartleys' party, determined to renew acquaintance with him, and, if she could, discover more of his home and background.

This renewal of acquaintance proved remarkably easy, for immediately on entering the Hartleys' large high-ceilinged drawing room among the later arrivals, Edward Keithley having been detained on matters pertaining to his country estate, she found Hugh De Brandon at her side. Discouraging, in his sardonic, high-handed manner, others who had gathered about her, he escorted her to a convenient chair, brought her a glass of champagne, then sat himself, slightly uncomfortably, on a delicate, spindly affair opposite her. In other circumstances she might have been offended at this high-handedness, but as things were, it suited her well enough, so she smiled her warm smile, and fell, remarkably easily, into a general conversation with him, during which she managed to elicit the information that his estate in Lancashire was obviously a considerable one, and his house large, inconvenient, and rambling so that, since he was relatively seldom there, only one wing of it was occupied. This so fell in with her Gothic imaginings that a wave of hysterical laughter threatened to overcome her, but she sternly averted such a catastrophe, and next moment all amusement left her, as Mr. De Brandon said sadly with a strange bitter regret, "It was not so but two years ago, when my wife Elizabeth was alive! Then we had friends, and almost up to the last were forever entertaining, the visitors' wing constantly occupied, and everything always a bustle. . . ."

He stopped, and such an expression of pain crossed his face, giving it an open, unguarded look, as to sober her completely; and she chided herself for so wantonly inviting confidences that she knew he would not readily give, and that she did not in reality wish to receive. She had, she felt, been sly in encouraging him to talk by showing *concern,* where all she really felt was curiosity. But it was too late to withdraw now, and she must sit, uncomfortably aware of her own shortcomings, listening to his seemingly nostalgic references to happier days, and worse, to his daughter's far happier earlier childhood: at six years old, Amelia had obviously been the apple of everyone's eye, gay, pretty, even, perhaps, a little spoiled. But then, Harriet inferred, Mr. De Brandon's wife had begun to monopolize his thoughts. Though he in no way embarrassed her with confidences—indeed, only made a bleak reference to Elizabeth's disliking Lancashire, tiring of the country, and being always anxious for London—Harriet detected a tension, the beginnings of dissension in the home. It was obvious; and that this state of affairs became rapidly worse seemed certain, for Hugh De Brandon's brow darkened, and saying suddenly, with a hard laugh, that he pitied women with their pathetic empty ambitions, their simple desires and uncomplicated romantic notions, always subservient to the wishes, the whims, the unkindnesses of their menfolk, got up as abruptly as he had first arrived, and with a brief bow, moved away.

Reflecting wryly that she must look rather ridiculous, seated opposite a patently empty chair and clutching half a glass of wine, and that this was entirely her own fault, that she deserved to find herself in such a situation, Harriet rose as soon as she might, and made her way over to

Anne and other friends. Here, the unwanted confidences, and her part in causing them, were temporarily forgotten, and she spent, as always, a thoroughly enjoyable and satisfactory evening.

CHAPTER V

Once home, however, Harriet's conscience began to trouble her again, and also, perhaps illogically in the circumstances, Hugh De Brandon's final cavalier treatment of her began to rankle. If *she* was a meddler, *he* was certaily ill bred, a boor to leave her so, and eventually working up a comfortable indignation, Harriet resolved to become involved with Mr. De Brandon and his affairs no more. She rose next morning confirmed in this resolve, and set off in the carriage about ten of the clock with her aunt for the Circulating Library on Bond Street. But here, to her fury, her resolution was immediately broken by meeting Hugh De Brandon himself at the very door of the Library, and being forced, in common civility, to introduce him to Miss Neligan. The bright, birdlike features of the elderly lady lit up at once, and always friendly, she exerted herself to be even more so. To Harriet's surprise, Mr. De Brandon gave her all his attention. His manner a mixture of sincere interest and discreet deference to her age, he stood with them for nigh on ten minutes before going on his way, and on his departure, Miss Neligan said gleefully, "Now *that's* a nice fellow. I know; I can always tell when some of these young bucks are but *pretending* to be nice to me, and when they are really so!"

Harriet replied, with uncustomary tartness, for she felt rather put out, that Mr. De Brandon, being a well-turned thirty and more, could hardly be called a "young buck," at which her aunt gave a near eldritch cackle of laughter and replied, a little maliciously, that she had best beware about relegating such people to the corridors of crabbed age, since Harriet would soon find herself among them. And on her aunt's then adding, a little wistfully, that when one was seventy, thirty-odd looked enticingly young, Harriet's heart smote her, and tucking her arm warmly through the stringy, elderly one, she said contritely, "I'm sorry, my dear! I am a little put out this morning, but that is no excuse for behaving in so surly a manner to you! I beg you will forgive me, and let me help you search for a really *Gothic* romance!"

As Miss Neligan's penchant for blood-curdling novels was the joke of her friends, good-humor was restored at once, and the two women entered the Library in the greatest amity.

They found Selina with some of her young friends, and Mr. Huntley in attendance, there before them, and as Selina welcomed Miss Neligan with all her usual affection, their search for a novel was again delayed. Harriet, standing a little apart, watching with great contentment her loved ones so warmly disposed to each other, was suddenly aware of the considering gaze of Mr. Huntley himself and another young gentleman of the party whom she recognized, with something of a shock, as one of the rather obnoxious dandies who had discussed her brother some evenings ago. It was obvious that Mr. Huntley, at least, was concerned whether to speak to her on some matter or not, and intuitive as well as quick-witted, Harriet wondered at once if this might pertain to her brother's affairs, especially since the unknown young man, whom she knew to have been lately in Rome, was looking at present remarkably embarrassed and apprehensive. Mentally approving the delicacy of Mr. Huntley's behavior, which showed a sense of duty battling with one of decorum, she moved over to where the two of them stood, and said, pleasantly, "Mr. Huntley, I beg you will introduce me to your friend, for I believe him to be but recently returned from Italy where, as you know, my brother Geoffrey is presently living."

She understood Mr. Huntley to mutter, but so low as not to be clearly heard, that the gentleman in question was no friend of his, an acquaintance only, being a ramshackle fellow, but he had, all the same, news of Sir Geoffrey. He introduced his companion and then fell silent, looking in a somewhat commanding manner at the other, who gazed back in obvious trepidation. Impatient, suddenly, of their extreme youth and of the gaucherie, at least of the traveler, Harriet said briskly, "Well, and what is this news, if you please?"

The young dandy, who had been introduced as Viscount Wynter (and thus identified by Harriet as the younger sprig of a somewhat elderly roué with more money than decorum), cleared his throat nervously and replied that he had just heard, from another friend of his, returned from Rome but yesterday, that Sir Geoffrey was in some difficulty regarding a duel. Here he broke off, but on Harriet's agitatedly inquiring for details, especially if this had already taken place, and if so, was her brother, at least, unharmed, added hastily, by way of comfort, "No—at least not before my friend's departure; and that is the problem, you see. The duel—an affair of the heart, you understand—could not take place as . . . as Sir Geoffrey was, in the interim, taken to prison for a debt or wager, or some such that he could not fulfill. And so he has, as it were, two affairs of honor on his hands. Neither of which," he concluded, with a scared look at Harriet's face, "he can, at the moment anyway, discharge."

Harriet's heart sank, and although never given over to the vapors like so many of her sex, she yet felt an unsteadiness and trembling in her limbs. Mr. Huntley, quick to notice this, took her arm firmly and escorted her solicitously to one of the sensible chairs the Library afforded, and naturally, in doing so, attracted the notice of the rest of the party. Miss Neligan and Selina, both with great good sense and alacrity, attended to her, Miss Neligan producing her vinaigrette, without which she never traveled, and Selina loosening the ribbons of Harriet's bonnet. But pushing these kindly helpers away, impatient with herself for her weakness when there was so much to be considered, Harriet asked Mr. Huntley to be so good as to summon the carriage to take her home and, on this arriving with great promptitude, hustled both Selina and her aunt inside with her. Mr. Huntley collected his mare, which had been tethered to the mounting block nearby, and the rest of the company, aware of some drama, but not yet of its nature, melted discreetly away.

On the journey back to Park Lane, Harriet's mind traveled round like the proverbial squirrel in its cage. The duel could, alas, be easily explained; the imprisonment for nonfulfillment of a debt, if simply that, could not. Her brother was rich, and his bankers in Italy capable as well as impeccable. Even if temporarily embarrassed for some reason—a debt incurred elsewhere in the country, perhaps—the problem would be of short duration. It could be that this, indeed, was the case, and the matter had been resolved immediately after Viscount Wynter's friend's departure. But somehow it did not sound as if the solution were destined to be such a happy one. And if not, it stood to reason that deliberate intrigue and malice were involved. She shuddered, and at last aware of the importunities of her companions, told them briefly of Geoffrey's situation.

The carriage being now at the door, Harriet descended at once, and leaving Mr. Huntley, dismounting from his mare, to hand the other two down, hurried at once into the house in search of Edward. Alas, her spirits were thrown into a further turmoil by the butler's announcing that Mr. Keithley had left unexpectedly and urgently some half-hour ago for his country estate, the business that had made them late for the Hartleys' rout recurring, and this time necessitating his immediate presence in the country for, he had surmised, at least a sennight. Even Anne was from home, to spend the day with friends at Richmond, and Harriet, a prey to near despair, clenched her hands and strove to think and plan rationally. She was standing thus, collecting her thoughts, when Miss Neligan entered the room. Having been made privy by the butler to Mr. Keithley's departure, she had advised Selina and Mr. Huntley to stay discreetly away from the drawing room at present, and had sought Harriet at once. Now seeing her niece's rigid back and nervous air, she said gently, "You must not fret yourself in this way, my dear. There is nothing to be done at the moment, with Edward from home . . . as a woman you cannot contrive alone in such a situation!"

On Harriet's returning her no answer, she added a little diffidently that perhaps they could send a message to Edward, "For he is always so kind and reliable, and would undoubtedly cut his visit short as he might to come back and advise you what is to be done."

"What useful advice can he give!" replied Harriet very low, "with Geoffrey so far distant? . . . Even supposing I felt able to claim his time in such a way!"

"He has always been Geoffrey's friend—"

"Yes!" said Harriet fiercely. "Always pulling him out of scrapes, patching matters up, setting things to rights, eternally hoping for some improvement of character—almost as often as I myself! Enough is enough! There comes a time when he must not be permitted to involve himself further!"

Miss Neligan considered her niece compassionately. She knew Harriet's nature, and what must now be her immediate desire, to be doing something, *anything*, to help her brother's situation. She broached, therefore, the idea that had entered her mind immediately on hearing Edward Keithley to be from home.

"In Edward's absence—and whether you relent and send him a message or not, there must be *some* delay before his return—I can think of no better able to advise you than Mr. De Brandon. Indeed, since he claims acquaintance with Geoffrey in Italy, he may well be able to guess at some of the people involved, and so you might at least, by Edward's return, have the story a little more coherent." Warming to her suggestion, she concluded,

"Why, he could perhaps inquire of Mr. Huntley's young friend and collect more details—names and so on!"

A sudden image of Hugh De Brandon rose in Harriet's distressed mind, his occasional flashes of sincerity; the glimpse she had had of unhappiness, despair even, in his eyes; the impression of strength, whether for good or evil, he always gave. She turned and looked hopefully at her aunt, only to say despondently, within the space of a minute, "I cannot; I hardly know him . . . and besides, I . . . I do not like him."

"I never, *never* thought to hear such foolishness from *you*! Here is a desperate situation, your brother possibly in need of help no woman is capable of giving; Edward gone from home perhaps for *days*: you with no relative, or anyone close to you to aid you . . . and you refuse to help the only way you can, because you do not *like* someone!"

Harriet flushed, but answered steadily enough, "Besides, he is very much occupied with his own affairs, and—and I do not think he would be sufficiently interested to help me in mine. Indeed, to my mind he would intensely dislike being asked—"

"You know your own affairs best, of course, but I think you are wrong. Anyway, we shall not know till we try. He can but refuse. And," finished Miss Neligan stoutly, "if *you* will not ask him, I vow I will!"

"He may have left London."

"Nonsense. How can you say so? It is but an hour since we were with him on Bond Street!"

Harriet realized that, in her distress and shock, she had actually forgotten this, and sensibly deciding that she was probably in a less fit state emotionally to make reasonable decisions than her aunt, and moreover no other suggestion presenting itself, she agreed at least to approach Mr. De Brandon, taking Miss Neligan as chaperon, and ask his advice.

Leaving the drawing room to put this unnerving decision into practice at once, they found Selina and Mr. Huntley hovering in the outer hall, concerned and anxious to help in any way possible. But Mr. Huntley, although all that was kind and reliable, was too young to be of much real help, and as for Selina—even in the midst of her worries, Harriet looked narrowly at her, fearful lest Geoffrey's predicament was causing her renewed pain. But the clear blue ingenuous eyes were obviously solicitous for Harriet alone, and so, breathing an inward sigh of relief, she thanked the two young people, and begging their discretion, at least for the moment, explained that she was but now on her way to someone whom she thought could be of help. She then ordered the carriage, and remembering hearing Mr. De Brandon's house to be at the far end of Mount Street, away from the Park, set off thither without delay.

They had almost reached their destination when, to their consternation, they saw Mr. De Brandon himself, driving a light phaeton and turning toward the Park. Harriet called to the coachman and fortunately, this worthy halting the horses with some flurry, Mr. De Brandon's attention was drawn to them. Seeing the anxious faces at the carriage window, he in his turn reined in, and telling his tiger to stand to the horses, jumped down and came across to them. Harriet felt a moment of uncharacteristic panic, and even as she fought it, she heard her aunt say determinedly, "Mr. De Brandon, I am too old to let convention trammel me, and you seem to be a man of good sense, so I tell you directly that my niece is in a

pickle"—here she paused, and ignoring Harriet's horrified
gaze, went on—"or rather, her *brother* is in a pickle.
And with Mr. Keithley from Town with business at his
Surrey estate, you but recently come from Italy, and the
matter being urgent, I persuaded her to come to you."

Confusion, followed by a glimmer of amusement, flick-
ered across the sardonic features, although Mr. De Brandon was careful to keep his eyes fixed on Miss Neligan's
face, presumably so as to a little lessen Harriet's embarrassment, if that were possible. But her aunt had not finished. Taking a deep breath, she continued, in her high,
precise, elderly voice, "*I* am come as chaperon. I tell you
frankly, I had far rather be elsewhere, and I think Harriet
would do better to explain matters without my presence.
But I am not so completely lost to convention as not to
see it would be not quite the thing for her to visit your
house unattended."

At this Harriet, who had never, in years, found herself
so totally bereft of speech, opened her mouth to inter-
vene, but was this time forestalled by Mr. De Brandon,
who replied, still avoiding her eye, and giving all his
courteous attention to Miss Neligan, "Perhaps, for everyone's ease, Lady Frome would join me for a drive?" and
turning his attention at last to Harriet, explained, "You
have no fear, I know of phaetons . . . and there is nothing,
you will agree, in the least exceptionable in the two of us
driving in the Park. It is not now the fashionable hour,
and we should, I think, contrive to be sufficiently
private."

Partly from fear of what her eccentric aunt would say
next if she were a party to any explanation of the affair,
and feeling therefore that she could best manage alone,
Harriet agreed to this suggestion, and was soon up beside

Mr. De Brandon in the phaeton, her aunt returning alone in the carriage to Park Lane.

Once in the Park, however, fortunately at this hour as sparsely populated as Mr. De Brandon had surmised, she found herself at a loss how to broach the matter, rehearsing various openings in her mind, all of which she felt would not at all do. After driving thus some little time in silence, Mr. De Brandon took matters into his own hands, and glancing sharply sideways at the averted profile, said quite gently, "I realize you are here by your aunt's maneuverings. Will you not make the best of it and tell me what is troubling you? I collect it concerns Sir Geoffrey, and as he and I have Italian acquaintances in common, suspicion that is why your aunt thought I might be of use."

Grateful for his kindliness in making any confidences easier for her, Harriet shook off her embarrassment, agreed that her aunt's reasoning had been as he surmised, and apologizing for approaching him, a comparative stranger, with her problems, told him briefly of what had occurred that morning, and what she had chanced to overhear a week earlier. Mr. De Brandon looked grave, and after a slight hesitation, said firmly, "This is a time to speak frankly, so I must beg your forgiveness in causing you pain. From what he has told me of his past history, I do not think it will come as a shock to you to know your brother to be at best notoriously indiscreet, even in a Society as lax as that of Rome. . . ." He went on dryly, "I have no quarrel with what would conventionally be called, I am sure, *wild*, perhaps even *sinful* behavior, but I do not tolerate ill breeding. And even during my stay Geoffrey had passed what I considered to be the bounds of decent behavior."

Feeling with some force that wild behavior was in itself ill bred, Harriet was nevertheless too disturbed to take issue on this, only begging her companion to be more specific. Mr. De Brandon scanned her face with concern, and went on in a voice in which diffidence and compassion were equally blended, "At the time of my visit, Geoffrey was—involved—with a young countess, very beautiful, and very silly, the wife of an old, proud, Roman noble. . . . To steal a wife's affections from a young man is one thing. To flaunt her indiscretions in the face of an elderly, dignified husband powerless to hold her is another. . . . I suspicion Sir Geoffrey is now reaping the reward of his cruelty."

Harriet stared at him in horror. "You *know* this husband?"

"If my suspicions are correct, I am acquainted with him, yes. And I would hazard this is the kind of revenge his devious mind would arrange."

"But surely, he is too old to duel?"

Mr. De Brandon smiled, not pleasantly. "He has influence, and friends. It would not be difficult to contrive some quarrel with a younger man . . . a good duelist."

Harriet gave a faint exclamation, and found Mr. De Brandon's arm supporting her. He said bitterly, "I vow I am beyond hope, thoughtless and inconsiderate still! I should have told you more gently! I beg you will forgive me!"

Harriet rallied at once, replying firmly that indeed he had done best to tell her directly and without false comfort. She then turned to look him fully in the face, and asked, endeavoring to keep any quaver from her voice, though she suspicioned already what the answer would be, "And the imprisonment for debt?"

"Is probably a turn of the same screw if, as I collect, however heavy his gambling debts, your brother is always in a position to pay them?"

On Harriet's agreeing this to be so, they fell silent, both busy with their thoughts, hers concerning her brother's continued shortcomings, his on how best to help her. At last, pursuing her train of thought aloud, determined still to make excuses for him, though she knew these to be futile, she said sadly, "He was so kind, so anxious to please, when he was younger, you know ... with me, at least. But his father gave him no chance to develop such gentle traits. He was always adjuring him, even when Geoffrey was but in short coats, to *achieve* something, *ordering* his interests in matters which held no appeal for him, never loving or tolerant—"

Hugh De Brandon replied gravely, with no hint of mockery or impatience, "My dear Lady Frome, from what I have heard, I deduce he has since had many chances to reform. You, above all, have had endless patience with him, but you must now accept the fact that it is impossible he will change. At first, perhaps, with his father, your argument in his favor might have had some substance; but for many years now, no such excuse can be made for him, rather the contrary."

Through her heartache, she said, in some surprise, "But how is it you know so much about him?"

He replied dryly, "People talk, you know. And in our close Society here in London, you and I have, of necessity, many acquaintances in common. Besides, Geoffrey himself, in Italy told me something of—"

Here he broke off in some confusion, but not before Harriet had remembered the cynical observations, at their first meeting, of the man now seated beside her. Already distressed, she now felt herself almost overset, wondering how she came to be here, confiding her worries to such a man. So that, struggling with her emotions, she at first only half heard Mr. De Brandon saying anxiously, "I beg you will not worry so. If you will permit me, I think I can be of help since it happens I am committed to visit Italy at the end of next week."

At this, Harriet's head came up, and seeing the look of doubt as well as hope on her face, he continued, with obvious amusement, "I assure you, my passage is already certain on the packet, and my place already secure in the diligence at Calais. I should then be in Rome within little more than a sennight, and will at once endeavor to ascertain what has occurred, and if possible put matters to rights."

In her relief Harriet forgot all her recent renewed dislike of Mr. De Brandon, all reservations she held about his character, all her embarrassment for her own, and her aunt's, present behavior. She turned a radiant face toward him, and, now the stress was to some extent over, felt unwanted tears of relief filling her eyes. Because of these, she did not remark the look of pain and withdrawal on Hugh De Brandon's own countenance as he returned her gaze, or the sudden hardening of his expression. She said, tremulously, all that was proper, only adding that she hoped her affairs would not too much incommode him, or place him awkwardly *vis-à-vis* his friends. Something of her private opinion of the probable nature of these friends must have been implicit in her manner, for he said swiftly, "Not at all: I am certain of their help." And then, in so toneless a voice as to convey his disapproval, "A great many of them, you know, are in fact very kind, having only *different* moral values from those of our English Society, rather than none at all . . . and some of those values often far more tolerant and humane than ours!"

He continued, as Harriet, her cares momentarily forgotten, looked at him thoughtfully, "As for the few others, the abandoned, even the depraved, well, I should tell you I often find them vastly amusing and good company! But unlike your brother, I hope I know how, while enjoying them, to keep my moral distance, and not become tainted by their—unpleasantnesses."

Realizing from this remark that many of Geoffrey's shortcomings, or worse, had not been spoken of, and aware of the delicacy that avoided any mention of them, Harriet could only repeat her indebtedness to Mr. De Brandon, adding she knew not how she would have gone on without his help. This put her in mind of Edward again, and she was about to suggest she might also at least ask his advice when she was forestalled by her companion, who observed sensibly that he would prefer consulting with Mr. Keithley for his opinion also, and he would therefore, with Harriet's permission, take a turn down to Surrey tomorrow to acquaint Edward Keithley with the matter and obtain his views. Indeed, he added, if she and her aunt would like to accompany him, it would perhaps be even better, as she herself could then seek Edward's advice at first hand. He finished by saying that his visit must be made no later than tomorrow, however, as within two days he was engaged to drive his daughter and her governess back to Lancashire.

Harriet, gratefully accepting this offer, observed in some surprise, "Your daughter is here in London, then?"

"Yes. She arrived unexpectedly with her governess but yesterday . . . the woman had some foolish fears on account of Amelia's increasing tendency toward bad nightmares, even sleepwalking, and while not wishing to accept responsibility for this, yet being naturally loath to leave the child behind, brought her with her to London in the cumbersome traveling coach we never now use. . . . She would have done better to remain at home than risk an accident on the road, foolish woman." He added flatly, "I do not like my daughter in London."

Something in his manner restrained Harriet from further questioning, and she was about to ask Mr. De Brandon to be so good as to drive her back to Park Lane when he said, abruptly and with some awkwardness of manner, "I have no right to ask it of you . . . but I suppose I could not prevail on you to call at Mount Street with me now and meet Amelia? Her governess is there, and so there could be nothing exceptionable in your doing so."

And as Harriet, a little astonished at this sudden request, hesitated to answer, he went on swiftly, "But that was both foolish and selfish of me! You have so much of your brother's affairs to occupy your thoughts—"

"No, indeed, there is nothing to be done immediately, and you have been so good as to ease my mind considerably. I should be pleased to make your daughter's acquaintance."

Hugh De Brandon smiled at her then, with a curious shy vulnerability, saying apparently by way of explanation, "She is so much alone, you know, and although a good woman, her governess has little to recommend her as feminine company!" His eyes taking in, in an experienced manner, Harriet's pelisse of green figured silk with piped oversleeves, and her matching bonnet, he went on obliquely, "As a little girl of six—indeed, almost before she was out of leading strings—she had an eye for clothes, and would always want the prettiest dresses to wear."

"But not now?"

"No." He sighed. "She is very much changed, always so strange and quiet. But"—rallying—"perhaps if she could meet sometimes with livelier company she might, in time, improve!"

"She has no friends of her own age?"

"Regrettably no. In Lancashire we are rather isolated and solitary; and, as you will guess, here in London I have very few friends with young families. . . . Besides, I will not, as I have said already, have her in Town."

Wishing to ask him whether this was because a young child would hamper his sophisticated amusements, or for some more worthy reason such as her health, Harriet contented herself with saying mildly that all children, especially little girls, were normally sociable beings, and perhaps Amelia's isolation was responsible for her being so changed and for her more recent nightmares. She naturally made no mention that the lack of a mother was almost certainly the root cause, and it was left to Mr. De Brandon to observe, as he had previously implied, that with her mother's death Amelia's whole character had changed, and unaccountably remained so, time having had no healing effect, as one would have expected.

At this moment they reached an archway leading to a paved courtyard and Mr. De Brandon's house. The phaeton swept beneath the arch, and dismounting, the owner gave his hand to Harriet and escorted her through the heavy main door, already opened by a very correct servant. Inside, all was rich, somber. The vast hall was dark with heavy paneling; and no lighter touch, flowers perhaps, or a book, an embroidery frame, even a shawl thrown casually down, were to be seen about the salon into which she was ushered. Still less was there any evidence of a child in the house. No sudden voices, no rush to greet a father, no puppy or recent plaything momentarily overlooked by the servants. Just a heavy silence that had something depressing in it. Harriet gave herself a mental shake, and refusing Mr. De Brandon's offer of refreshment, listened to his directing a servant to fetch Miss Phipps and Amelia to the salon at once. A few minutes later, footsteps sounded in the hall, one set heavy, the steps of cumbersome middle age; the other light, certainly, but curiously subdued. Harriet waited, a little apprehensively now, for the child to appear.

CHAPTER VI

The diminutive figure, standing beside a comfortable woman of about forty-five clad in black bombazine, seemed insubstantial, a little ghost. Her fair, wispy hair, well brushed, hung to her narrow shoulders; her arms, and her legs from the calf down (for she was clad in childish petticoats), were like matchsticks; her feet, encased in soft black pumps, overlong and thin. The small pointed face, with its narrow chin the only feature, it seemed, that resembled her father, was pale, almost sallow, and the eyes, steadily regarding Harriet, a smoky gray. There was no open innocence in that look, but a guarded appraisal almost; and not once, so far, had she glanced at her father.

"Say good afternoon, Amelia," instructed her governess

in the rather wheezy, squeaky tones of the overweight, but quite kindly.

"Good afternoon, Ma'am, Papa," said the colorless little voice, while the eyes, now, were downcast.

Harriet, sorry for any small creature so bereft of life, said gently, in her warm voice, "How do you do, Amelia, I am *very* glad to make your acquaintance."

She would have liked to have remarked on the prettiness of the child's gown, or some such thing, but as she was clad in pale yellow, a color singularly unbecoming to a sallow complexion, wisely forebore any false compliment.

To this kindly speech Amelia gave no answer, gave no sign, indeed, of having heard, and Mr. De Brandon, patently ill at ease in the face of his daughter's vast reserve, asked awkwardly, yet with tenderness, if she had been good and learned her lesson today. The child instantly, at the sound of his voice, looked away and down, and replied monosyllabically, "Yes," so that her father, glancing at the governess, inquired, "She is coming along better, Miss Phipps?"

"Oh yes, indeed, Mr. De Brandon. She is very quick, you know, when she wishes, and"—turning to Harriet— "if *only* she would be a little less indifferent and attend more to what I say, she could, I believe, be quite exceptional."

Waiting only for Hugh De Brandon to introduce her formally, Harriet asked, "Her attention is always elsewhere?"

"Well," replied Miss Phipps, glancing down at the bent head beside her, "I'd be more inclined, Lady Frome, to say her attention is *nowhere,* rather. She is so listless."

Under the scrutiny of these grown-ups, the bent head

never moved, the thin hand, held in the governess's large, well-covered one, remained as limp as ever. Mr. De Brandon, perhaps as well aware as Harriet that they had fallen to discussing the child as if she were not, indeed, present, leaned suddenly forward, and putting out his hand, said encouragingly, "Well, perhaps there has been too much work, and not enough amusement! Now that you *are* in London, shall I take you for a drive this afternoon?"

But it was an effort for him to finish his sentence, for the effect of both his gesture and his voice on Amelia was immediate and electric. She stepped back and away, her whole body tense. Shocked beyond words, Harriet looked up instantly into Hugh De Brandon's face, only to see sadness and resignation mixed with a hard smothered anger there, but no surprise. The governess, too, showed no alarmed concern, only shaking her head somberly at her employer. Mr. De Brandon turned away to the window, and glancing but once at his rigid back, Miss Phipps said in disapproving, yet resigned, tones, "Come along, Amelia." She nodded pleasantly to Harriet, and sedately marched her young charge from the room.

With the click of the salon door, silence fell. Harriet, regarding the unmoving figure still turned away from her, the hands clasped behind, the stiff set of the shoulders, said with compunction, "Children have these strange moods, you know. This will pass, I feel sure."

"I think not," replied Mr. De Brandon harshly. "She has been thus these two years."

"Since her mother's death?" said Harriet gently.

"Yes. Almost as if she were *afraid* of me—"

Remembering the swift impression she had gained of some cringing quality in the child's recoil, Harriet shuddered, and there crept quite unbidden into her mind Jane

Bentley's dangerous gossip of unhappiness and cruelty during the wife's lifetime, and Hugh De Brandon's own reference to his moods, his unkindness, his thoughtlessness. Even as she remembered all this, Mr. De Brandon turned his darkling arrogant face toward hers and fell to studying her silently. Fearing her thoughts, doubts rather, to be mirrored in her face, and resenting the ill-bred, unwavering regard, she began to gather up her reticule and the long embroidered scarf-shawl she had laid aside on entering the room, and saying her aunt might well wonder what had become of her, prepared to take her leave. But something in his expression, which had changed imperceptibly from close scrutiny to an incoherent, unspoken appeal, arrested her, and she said, impulsively, "Will she not *tell* you—no, that is foolish of me!—I would say, have you no notion what makes her thus? If you could but find the answer, you might well know then the cause of her sudden hysteria as well!"

"Yes," he replied flatly, "I have more than a notion!" And then, bitterly, "I am not a nice person to know, Lady Frome . . . I have no patience, and an insufferable—ungovernable—temper. I will bid you good day." He turned to open the door for her, and then, glancing at her expression, said contritely, "I am also a boor, Lady Frome. I should thank you for attempting to encourage my—intractable, unforgiving, timid—little cub; I should have known it would be of no use."

Harriet, accustomed for many years to patient struggles with Geoffrey's sulks and tantrums when a child, said impulsively, "Oh, but we have not tried sufficiently! It is not in my stubborn nature to throw my hand in yet! If I might suggest you bring her to Surrey with us tomorrow? It will be a change for her to be in company other than that of her governess. . . . Indeed, perhaps Selina will agree to traveling with my aunt and myself. She is a little nearer in age to Amelia, and a lighthearted companion these days. She could push her on the garden swing, and keep her amused while we discuss Geoffrey's predicament with Edward!"

With this speech, all her own worries again assailed her, and she fell silent, while Hugh De Brandon stared stiffly down at her, through her, it seemed, his dark brows drawn together. Then, at last, giving her his hand, he smiled suddenly, a totally unexpected, charming smile. "Who knows? Perhaps it would help. And I thank you very much for your suggestion."

The hour of departure having been set early, as they had more than a twenty-mile drive from Town into the heart of Surrey, the next day saw the party well on the road by ten of the morning. Inside the Keithleys' carriage, Anne sat with Harriet, Selina, and Amelia, Miss Neligan having ceded her place so that Anne, returned from Richmond the previous evening, might have the opportunity of a sight of her husband, perhaps even, with his agreement, remain in the country with him. Alongside, Mr. De Brandon, astride his favorite saddlehorse, a fastidious high-spirited creature, cantered as outrider. The morning was fresh, and the well-wooded hillsides, mantled in rain-washed green and still scattered with splashes of blossom, white, pale pink, and magenta, were a sight to lift the saddest heart. Despite her worries, Harriet felt refreshed, and glancing sideways at the silent child, dressed today in a coat of powder blue better suited to her pale countenance, and with a small, close-fitting bonnet hiding the wispy hair, said gently, "Is it not pretty here? And when you reach Mr. Keithley's, you will find the gardens quite beautiful."

"There are peacocks, you know," added Selina encouragingly, eager for all the world, even this silent unattractive child, to be as happy as she now was herself. "And a garden swing, which I will swing for you, if you would like it."

The child looked expressionlessly at each of them in turn, and then said, very low to Selina, that when she was very little, she, too, had a swing in her garden. But, she added, it had long gone.

That she had spoken at all was encouraging, and Harriet silently congratulated herself for inviting Selina, and was grateful too for Selina's good nature in agreeing to travel with them instead of spending the day at her fiancé's house as had been planned. In point of fact, it had been Mr. Huntley himself who was responsible for this decision, his concern for Harriet's predicament moving him to do all he could to accommodate her, and Selina, wishing to stand well in her fiancé's eyes, agreeing to help in any way she could.

All further attempts to draw the child out failed, however, so that Anne and Harriet spoke at random together, both privately preoccupied with concern for Geoffrey's affairs, and Selina, finding her good offices not appreciated by Amelia, fell rather sulkily silent. Mr. De Brandon's profile, glimpsed intermittently at the side of the carriage, was also grimly thoughtful, so that it was a rather subdued party, despite the bright weather, that arrived finally at Mr. Keithley's.

They were, of course, unexpected, and consequently a great flurry arose on their arrival. Edward was delighted to see his wife, and, always fond of Harriet and protective toward Selina, made the entire party welcome, a few words sufficing for the moment to give the reason for the visit. The housekeeper quickly prepared a hasty nuncheon for the now rather weary travelers, and afterward Selina, her good humor quite restored by cakes, fruit, ratafia, and the obvious approval of Edward Keithley, whom she still held rather in awe, went willingly into the garden to amuse Amelia, and Harriet, Edward, and Mr. De Brandon retired to the library, leaving Anne deep in domestic affairs with the housekeeper.

It took but little time to apprise Edward of Geoffrey's predicament, but far longer to decide how to proceed. The two men were agreed personal inquiry was far better in every way than letters by courier, and Mr. De Brandon having once again spoken of his intended visit to Italy the following week and offered his assistance, this was gratefully accepted. Harriet, fearing above all her own inaction, had made some tentative suggestion that she, too, visit Rome, suitably accompanied, but both men were so emphatic that this would not do that she was forced to give up the idea as useless. Mr. De Brandon engaged, then, immediately on his arrival in Rome, to inquire of his many friends details of the affair, Edward Kiethley and Harriet leaving to his discretion whether to do so privately or quite openly.

"I wager, you know, it will be open, for nothing is ever discreet there, but always picked over with relish, without even the pretense of privacy as here in England."

Although this was said in an aside to Edward, Harriet, at that moment walking about the room to ease her worry and frustration at her inadequacy, chanced to overhear, and her heart sank. She returned to the discussion, almost overset, to find the two men debating whether, before his departure, Mr. De Brandon should approach Mr. Huntley's acquaintance from Rome to try to glean more of the affair, and if possible identify the participants. This was indeed a problem. Selina's fiancé was without doubt a man of honor and discretion, but it did not seem the same could be said of his acquaintance. Finally, it was Harriet who announced impatiently that everything would be much farther forward if Mr. De Brandon did obtain some information on that score, and that for her part, she would prefer him to make such inquiries, and risk any subsequent gossip among the *ton*.

This having been agreed, the entire visiting party made some pretense of enjoying themselves, walking a little in the grounds, commenting on the knot garden, restored after many years of indifference to its former vivid, geometric beauty, and finally taking their leave. As Harriet had expected, Anne remained with her husband, so the carriage party now consisted of only herself, Selina, and Amelia. Both the younger occupants were silent, Amelia expressionless still, Selina's face a little flushed and sulky since, as she had managed to whisper before leaving to Harriet, her young charge had hardly spoken at all, and then only in colorless monosyllables. Even more annoying, and strange, for that matter, was that despite Selina's swinging her for long periods, showing her the miniature lake, the dovecotes, and the famous peacocks, she had appeared indifferent to everything.

"And I declare," Selina had concluded in low but fierce tones, "I am well nigh *exhausted* with pushing that swing, and tramping the grounds to amuse her!"

Harriet, feeling the other's complaints more than a little justified, had soothed her as best she could and resolved to trouble her no more on the morrow, but perhaps enlist her aunt's help in another scheme she had in mind.

Accordingly, on their arrival back at Mr. Keithley's house in Town she asked Mr. De Brandon, if he were not too pressed, to dismount and take a glass of wine with her aunt and herself, saying her personal maid could look after Amelia for a little. Mr. De Brandon, glancing keenly down at Harriet's upturned face, and sensing this to be more than formal courtesy, agreed, and was soon seated with the two ladies in the small salon. Fortunately, Miss Neligan, with her constant kind and harmless interest in other people, asked to be told about the visit and thus gave Harriet her looked-for opportunity to suggest that, since Mr. De Brandon would be occupied at least part of the morrow with Mr. Huntley's companion for Harriet's sake, she should take Amelia on an outing. "To Philip Astley's circus, perhaps, or to buy some really pretty stuff to make an elegant gown."

Mr. De Brandon said gravely, but with some irritation in his voice, "I fear her visit today was not a success. Your young friend took such trouble with her, all to no avail, and now *you* wish to saddle yourself with her tomorrow. It is a hopeless case, you know."

"Nevertheless, with your agreement I should like to try just once more. . . . I shall not trouble Selina again since"—with a swift smile—"she has had such a dose today, but perhaps my aunt would accompany us for a little while at least, and I will see what I can do!"

So it was settled that, the weather being fine, Mr. De Brandon's coach should deliver Amelia a little before eleven next morning.

CHAPTER VII

They went first, Harriet and Amelia alone since Harriet thought it too exhausting and dusty an expedition for Miss Neligan, to Astley's Circus and Menagerie. Harriet, watching the intent little face, feeling the previously submissive little hand tighten in hers, and discussing spasmodically the animals' natural haunts, was pleased to discern a lessening of that wariness, that almost tangible wall of restraint, that had earlier been so marked. Indeed, during one of the more spectacular equestrian acts, Amelia clasped her hands and gasped with delight, only wishing she could take one of the ponies home with her, but adding that she supposed Miss Phipps and the servants would not like it. Harriet learned that since her strange illness she had had no pony of her own, on the physician's advice.

"But have you no puppy or kitten to amuse you?"

Amelia shook her head.

"Perhaps I could ask your papa—"

The child looked up and said in a flat voice, yet with curious overtones, "Oh, my papa gave me one once ... but it—it did not suit. Still, my mother contrived to find it a nice home; one of the grooms took it for his daughter."

Her face then took on its closed, stony look again, and remained so for the rest of the visit. Harriet forbore to question her; she felt she would get further by accepting any such infrequent confidences without comment and ignoring the child's more usual air of seemingly unfriendly reticence, however tiresome that might be.

In the afternoon, her sympathy was again aroused and she had cause, ultimately, to congratulate herself on her earlier forebearance. They had had a light meal in the cool, walled garden at the rear of the house, with its single spreading beech tree, and Harriet proposed, before returning the child to her home, to drive to Bond Street (taking Miss Neligan with them, as she so loved to shop), to buy Amelia the tissue for a pretty, feminine gown, which could be run up that evening in no time, she knew, by Anne's sewing woman, and which any little girl, even the most self-contained, must love.

Accordingly, after having the seamstress take Amelia's measurements, and promising the child that the material she was about to choose would be made up, and the dress delivered to her father's house that very night, they set out for Bond Street.

They had entered the shop, and were already attended to by a hovering assistant, when Harriet became aware of the hard stare of a tall, commanding woman a little older than herself, and dressed in the height of fashion. On

Harriet's cool gaze washing over her face, the onlooker became momentarily a little discomposed, but rallying again swiftly, walked toward them with firm steps. Seen close, although the air of elegance remained, Harriet remarked the eyes to be beady-sharp, the large, rather fleshy nose to have an indefinably inquisitive droop, and the mouth to be hard and narrow, like a trap. She decided she did not at all like the newcomer, and was intending to give her the set-down of an unrecognizing stare when she was forestalled by the stranger saying in high, clear tones, "Now, I know we have not met, Lady Frome, but that is purely fortuitous. My name is Caroline Wentworth, we have many friends in common"—here she named a few—"but I am only just come to London, having spent the last few years in France with a sick husband, and previously being nigh on *buried* in Scotland!"

Harriet could not do otherwise than acknowledge this forthright speech gracefully, and feeling much put out, introduce Mrs. Wentworth and Miss Neligan, the latter, by the steely look in her eye, sharing Harriet's private opinion of the stranger. Mrs. Wentworth wasted but little time on Miss Neligan, however, whom she obviously considered, though a social equal, too old to bother with overmuch. Her eyes fell almost at once on Amelia, and she said, her manner an unpleasing blend of the abrupt and coy, "And I recognize *this* young person, too! Amelia De Brandon, is it not? She is *very* like her mother; indeed, the resemblance is uncanny!"

This was said with such point as to be impossible to miss, and made worse by being followed by the observation, seemingly musingly, "That is, when her mother was so distressed you know, and down in spirits, poor creature. . . . *Before* her marriage she was always far, far prettier than this little scrap will ever be!"

At the mention of her mother, Amelia turned first a deep, unbecoming red, and then whiter even than usual, looking pinched around the mouth, and almost physically ill. Her hand gripped Harriet's gloved one with painful intensity, and instinctively Harriet moved half in front of the small figure, saying firmly, "Aunt Marion, can you help Amelia decide on some material—the *very* prettiest—while Mrs. Wentworth and I talk a little?"

"Willingly," said her aunt grimly, giving Mrs. Wentworth's unconscious profile a very fierce scowl, and almost sweeping her little charge away from the large, firmly planted figure.

Left alone with her now seemingly dangerous new acquaintance, Harriet indulged herself in a wide stare and said blandly, "I fear I cannot remark any such resemblance, Madam, since I never knew Amelia's mother, and find, indeed, little about her to interest me in consequence."

Whatever else she might be, Mrs. Wentworth was not lacking in perception. Her mouth widened in an appreciative smile, but she said, nothing deterred, and with deliberate malice, "Oh, but you must not disclaim interest in her too quickly! *All* human relationships are interesting study, you know, especially marital ones . . . and with two such different temperaments, the one so pliant and innocently gay, the other, as you know, willful, dominant, insensitive, and impatient, the relationship was almost sure to be an uneasy one, and the outcome unhappy, to say the very *least*!"

Harriet, rendered nigh speechless at such ill breeding, so frank and crass a comment, unwomanly in every way, could only stare. Mrs. Wentworth had the grace to look a little embarrassed by the sense of outrage she had caused, but said in a disparaging manner, "Oh come, Lady Frome, we are both women of the world! There is no need for such missish airs between two people of our age and experience! Indeed, I spoke so partly to—to *warn* you a little. . . . In France, you know, there is a more practical attitude toward frank speaking, in that a kindly warning is considered more worthy than any overstrict observation of"—she hesitated, and concluded—"verbal etiquette."

It was not lost upon Harriet that somewhere her recent friendship with Mr. De Brandon had been remarked, and either by malice or foolishness, misinterpreted. She went hot with anger and embarrassment equally, but contrived to reply, her face expressionless and her manner like ice, "But we are not now in France, Mrs. Wentworth . . . I will bid you good day."

Mortified as she was beyond words, it took some time for Harriet's angry distress to lessen. She turned swiftly away, feeling forced to walk the length of the shop before crossing to where Miss Neligan and Amelia could be seen, both staring with apparent absorbed concentration at two lengths of material, one simple white cambric embroidered with tiny pink rosebuds, the other a very pale blue stuff, which would make up extremely elegantly for a little girl, perhaps with tiny puff sleeves and a tuckered neckline, with a velvet sash of deeper blue.

But on her coming up to them at last, both heads turned at once, Miss Neligan sharply taking in Harriet's heightened color and grim self-control, Amelia for once peering anxiously up at her, her small face set and white. Harriet felt this would not do. Firmly spreading out the lengths of stuff afresh, under the smiling eyes of the young shop assistant, she proceeded to attempt to discuss points of color and style with her companions, though she noticed that her young charge took no part in the debate. Miss Neligan rallying quickly, however, the business was soon concluded, and the party happily, to all outward appearances at least, left the shop, bearing not only the embroidered stuff, but a chip straw bonnet, with tiny pink rosebuds to match.

Because of the unpleasant Mrs. Wentworth, the visit to the shop had not been a success, however, and Harriet suspicioned that poor Amelia, however much she had wanted the dress on entering the shop, would now, if she wore it at all, never do so without remembering both the encounter, and her—what could it be, loneliness, distress at losing a beloved mother, or something more sinister, fear perhaps, or even panic? Harriet knew not; but that the child was seriously disturbed could not be denied. She would seem to fear her father; she would talk to no one; she had changed beyond recognition after her mother's death; and rumor had it that Mrs. De Brandon, bitterly unhappy with a husband overbearing and, on his own admission, evil-tempered, had eventually, somehow, died of her unhappiness. Harriet took herself to task for brooding, but think as she might, it was not a nice story, and while telling herself firmly that no one was ever made so miserable as to actually die of unhappiness, the alternatives of an accident caused by distress of mind, or a suicide even, were terrible to contemplate. No one, it would seem, knew the true facts; all was whispered innuendo; but that *something* had happened to provoke such gossip could not be denied.

With these ideas turning in her head, Harriet, stopping

at the Keithleys' only to set down Miss Neligan, who was tired after the expedition, drove on to take Amelia directly to her father's house. To her relief, Mr. De Brandon was still from home and they were received by the governess, all smiles at the gaily striped bandboxes, and telling Amelia what a fortunate child she was.

"Run upstairs, remove your cloak and bonnet, and wash your hands. Then come down to say your farewells and thank-yous to Lady Frome, child!"

Ordinarily, Harriet would have demurred, releasing the child from such formality and saying goodbye there and then. But her thoughts were too disturbed, and although refusing the governess's offer of refreshment, she decided to sit a little and await Amelia, trying meanwhile to ascertain something more about the child's earlier life from the pleasant woman before her.

But this idea was doomed to failure; the governess had not known Mrs. De Brandon, having been engaged by Amelia's father some two months after her death. The child had been then as she was today, silent and withdrawn save for her intermittent hysteria.

"Try as I may, Lady Frome, I cannot *reach* her! Nor find out why, suddenly, she becomes so upset. There seems to be no reason, or cause, for her outbursts," she said worriedly. "And more recently this new distress, these nightmares, and constant ramblings in her sleep! ... I know it is said sleepwalkers never fall, or harm themselves in any way, but what of chills taken from the night air, and suchlike? For I have twice found her outside the house, you know!"

Harriet sat, appalled.

"They are rather more recent, these nightmares and nightwalks, then?"

"Yes. I recollect she came running into the house the afternoon before the first bad dream, but once inside she was as quiet as usual, and gave no sign of any distress. Indeed, I only remember the incident because of the shockingly disturbed night that followed!"

Anxious for the child, and feeling that with so obviously sincere a person she could not call herself to task as a gossip, Harriet asked one of the questions uppermost in her mind as important.

"Mr. De Brandon is—understanding—with her? He does not seem much used to children."

"Indeed, he tries endlessly to win her confidence by kindness, but she is as close with him as with me; nothing gets past her guard or wins her heart." She sighed, and continued. "And I must admit for the past year at least, he has almost given up his attempts: he comes less and less to Hoyton Hall, and I for one cannot blame him. When he *is* there, he tries as hard as ever. But now, as well as distressing him, her obstinate reserve makes him angry inside. So, too, it would me, if I were her father. And he is not a man of easy temper, you know, Lady Frome, which makes such restraint more difficult for him."

At this point, rather to Harriet's relief since she now knew she would learn nothing of use or help to Amelia from Miss Phipps, and disliked gossip for gossip's sake, the child returned. She was walking in her precise fashion, across to the chair where Harriet was seated, when the door opened a second time, however, and Mr. De Brandon entered the room, a many-caped coat, despite the mild weather, still slung around his shoulders, and his hat carelessly held at his side. Ignoring Amelia, who hesitated, and then stood utterly still like a little wild creature, he said to Harriet, "Soames told me you were but now returned! I am come at once to thank you for putting up with my daughter an entire day!"

Feeling the sensibility of any daughter to be injured by such a remark, made as it was in all seriousness and with no trace of affectionate teasing, Harriet hastened to reply, "I have found her very pleasant company, and I hope she will tell you about all the animals we have seen at Astley's!"

As she said this, she instinctively put out her hand toward Amelia; and it was with a distinct shock of surprise that she found the child's cold one in hers. The face remained closed, the eyes downcast, but at least she was *there*, and Harriet, drawing her the merest fraction closer, thought she felt a slight tightening of the thin fingers around her own. It was a beginning, anyway, and she felt herself to be rather ridiculously elated.

This incident was not unremarked by Mr. De Brandon, and for a moment his dark inscrutable eyes rested on Harriet's own. Then, saying abruptly that Amelia must have her tea and be in bed betimes as they traveled north tomorrow, he dismissed Miss Phipps, too, with a brief word of thanks, and the two left the room, Harriet remarking sadly that father and daughter took not the least notice of each other.

It was obvious on their departure that Mr. De Brandon, while expressing his very real gratitude to Harriet, and observing that she appeared to have had an unwonted success with the child, did not intend to discuss Amelia further. Instead, he sat down opposite her (thus to her relief a little diminishing the overpowering presence he had created on his entrance, his tall figure made even taller by his long greatcoat) and said courteously, "As you know, I am taking Amelia home tomorrow, and I shall afterward drive down again within two days to post directly to Dover and the packet. I should thus be very shortly in Rome to attend as best I can to your brother's affairs."

Harriet could only murmur once again how much she was obliged to him.

"It is nothing; I should be there anyway. And I will send news as soon as I can."

He then again changed the subject by asking if she would be at Sir Henry Bohun's party that evening, and on her saying she must attend despite the Keithleys' absence, as the engagement had been a long-standing one and included Miss Neligan, he remarked with a sudden smile, "Well, I shall see you there!" And then, surprisingly, "We must have a pact, Lady Frome! No talk of our problems, yours or mine, tonight! We shall meet as carefree guests, and forget, for a short while all our *ennuis*."

"Willingly," said Harriet in her soft voice, giving Mr. De Brandon her usual warm smile.

That evening, therefore, Harriet found herself again in Mr. De Brandon's company. She had not sought it, preferring to tease her mind no more with uncomfortable mysteries, and knowing herself powerless to help Amelia further toward a happier childhood since she was to leave with her father for Lancashire at first light. It was a relief to meet with her pleasant, lighthearted friends, to dance a little, to discuss fashions, perhaps, with the women, and indulge in pleasant conversation with her often worldly, sophisticated, yet mostly good-natured beaux. Indeed, she viewed Mr. De Brandon's arrival with some sinking of the heart, and although immediately reproaching herself for this, since he was so good as to interest himself in Geoffrey's affairs for her sake, nevertheless had to force a smile on her lips as he came up to her.

He was dressed tonight with the utmost elegance, the exquisite cut of his black coat emphasizing the strength of his shoulders, his dark, saturnine countenance handsome above the crisp snowy folds of his cravat. Many heads turned toward him as he approached her to make his bow, and again soon after as he offered his arm to take her into supper, saying it was already quite late and she must be hungry. Annoyed with herself for not foreseeing the possibility of his asking her, and so arranging matters otherwise, Harriet could do no other than acquiesce gracefully, and leaving her immediate circle of friends, found herself in no time at all at a small table *tête-à-tête* with her uncomfortable partner. Looking narrowly at him, she thought to detect a gleam of mischief in his eye, and was sure of it when he said, in a dry voice, glancing swiftly round, "I fear we have given the gossips cause for thought ... I am not frequently so sociable, and you are always very much so, invariably surrounded by friends, so our exclusive preoccupation with one another must be— indeed is"—catching the gimlet eye of a large lady in purple—"considered worthy of comment!"

Harriet was amused in spite of herself. She had little time for those scandal-mongers who made bricks without straw, and knowing her behavior to have nothing reprehensible in it, enjoyed the speculation her unusual new friendship was causing. She said, an answering gleam of amusement in her own eyes, "You are away tomorrow, and will not have to listen to the whispered *on-dits*, or explain your uncharacteristic behavior, while I am in a very different case, remaining in Town!"

"Oh, you will contrive, Lady Frome, with your quick

wit and honeyed tongue! You know the rules of your small, polite world so well: you sanction its taboos, as the savages say, agree that goodness marches only with respectability and kindness with virtue—you will be a match for anyone who dares question *your* conduct ... yes, you will manage!"

This was said cynically, with a hard stare, and of a sudden Harriet felt a sharp stab of annoyance and exasperation. She said with some heat, "Mr. De Brandon, you have already ventured at an earlier meeting to criticize in an oblique manner what you imagine, because they are the generally accepted ones, to be *my* opinions on goodness and virtue. At the time, I was overset by news of Geoffrey, and too grateful for your help to take issue with you ... so I am still. But we are agreed tonight to forget such matters, so I beg *now* to point out that I am not one of those very young women, well schooled in behavior and still hiding behind their mamma's skirts, who know always right from wrong, who is good (and therefore acceptable), and who is bad (and therefore not), because their elders tell them so."

She paused a moment, but her companion making no comment, she continued. "It is a long time since I was very young, and indeed, I hope I was never missish. ... You do not have the prerogative, you know, of tolerance in the face of convention; and I would wager there are many of my sex who, if the truth were known, are far more understanding of peccadillos, vices even, than many men!"

"Bravo!" said Mr. De Brandon, with what Harriet chose to consider as condescension. Angry and mortified, she kept silence, resolving that he should not make her lose her temper further. But apparently unaware of her resentment, he continued thoughtfully. "You are an admirer, I take it, of the late Miss Austen, who never suffered slaves to convention amiably."

"To a degree, yes. In that she has a keen wit, and such a heroine as Elizabeth Bennet, or such pompous slaves to any society as Mr. Elton or Mr. Collins, are drawn deftly, the one with sympathy, the other two with deliberate clever malice. But"—here, she broke off to ask—"have you read *Mansfield Park*?"

"Indeed, yes."

"Well, what a *heroine* is Fanny Price! Silent to the point of being sly; sanctimonious; critical of any boldness or strength of character! I cannot think what Miss Austen could have been about to have so made her a heroine! Nor her pious Edmund a hero. In my opinion, they deserved one another!"

At this, Mr. De Brandon, laughing with genuine amusement, asked who, then, were Harriet's hero and heroine in the book.

"For, you know, a hero and heroine are the essential prerequisites of a good novel."

Harriet, by now laughing too, her natural good humor quite restored, replied, "Why, Mary and Henry Crawford, of course! What an agile mind and clear vision in the sister, yet kind, and tolerant, too, to true worth. Bearing with the insufferable Fanny's small-mindedness and priggish notions. . . . And as for the brother, Henry Crawford, I consider Fanny directly responsible for his fall; consider how long after his unworthy start, he paid sincere court to her, and the encouragement he received—only to have his hopes dashed at last. Indeed, it is worse than that, by far! For she refuses him; he accepts her refusal as honestly given, and turning to another woman in desperation, does finally trangress the bounds of propriety. And what does prim Miss Fanny observe? Not 'Poor fellow, I am, indirectly, the cause of all this,' or some such regret, but only, 'If he had waited a little, *I might have changed my mind.'* "

Harriet flushed, and stopped, aware her observations, being overemphatic, had carried her beyond the bounds of propriety, and Mr. De Brandon said quizzically, into the ensuing pause, "It would seem you believe a woman's 'yea' should be yea, and her 'nay,' nay, then!" And afterward with some feeling, "I believe you that your conception of true worth is not dictated by convention and that you would not so trifle with a man's affections . . . you are too honest."

This was too sudden, and brought Harriet up with a start, to an awareness of her surroundings. At a table nearby, several friends were eyeing her covertly, and further away, near the refreshment tables, a gentleman of her acquaintance turned away a moment too late in courteous embarrassment at having been observed to stare at her. She could not think what she had been about; the heat and intensity of her answers, indeed of her whole recent conversation, could easily be misinterpreted as real argument, and where it had been amusing to invite speculation on a slight friendship, it was quite another thing to be seen arguing with such fervor. Her eyes dropped, and she said hurriedly, with none of her usual poise, "Mr. De Brandon, I beg you will excuse me, but I should be grateful if you would escort me back to my party . . . I fear I am a little overcome by the heat; it is extraordinarily stuffy in here, is it not?"

Her companion was not deceived. He said ruefully, "I have caused you embarrassment . . . I should realize I am still looked at askance by some tabbies of my acquaintance. And by other people, too, for that matter. I should not have teased you so; I beg you will forgive me. But at least let me remark that it is refreshing to meet a woman of spirit, generosity, and beauty; and I fully concur about Miss Fanny Price!"

With this said half-humorously, he rose, and handing Harriet from the table, escorted her back to the ballroom without further conversation. On her way thither, her embarrassment was not lessened by the sight of Mrs. Wentworth arrayed strikingly in dark red, and sporting a handsome turban, whispering behind her fan, her eyes turned directly toward them.

For once the evening palled a little. Periodically, she glimpsed Hugh De Brandon's tall figure moving urbanely among the guests, dancing occasionally, sometimes talking, but never again approaching her circle. She appreciated his tact, and was grateful to him for it, yet could not but reflect that tomorrow he would be gone for some weeks, months even. Little by little, however, her friends claimed her attention again, for she could never be selfishly absorbed by her own thoughts for long, and indeed she was only recalled to the subject of Mr. De Brandon when her partner and host, Sir Henry Bohun, said with considerable diffidence during a cotillion, "Lady Frome, I hope you will not think me presumptuous, but I should beware of any—close friendship—with Hugh De Brandon! I know you have become acquainted but recently, or I would not presume to—to offer such advice."

As Harriet looked at him in considerable surprise, he went on hurriedly. "Forgive me, I have no right to interfere in your affairs, but I—I like and admire you deeply, and would not willingly have you unwittingly exposed to criticism by—uncharitable people."

Suppressing a strong desire to agree tartly that his interference was indeed both presumptuous and unwarranted, she raised her eyebrows a fraction and waited pointedly for him to explain himself, which he did by saying confusedly, "There was some scandal about his wife's death, you know. It was kept very close, and indeed, I know no details . . . but he was said to have been at least very cruel to her during her lifetime, and—and many people still look on him with disfavor."

Seeing the concern in the normally easy, good-humored countenance above her, and a little disturbed that the poised and detached Sir Henry Bohun should think the matter of such importance as to be prepared to risk embarrassment for her sake, Harriet softened; the hot retort about gossip and unwarranted criticism of her own conduct that rose to her lips remained unsaid, and instead she replied gently that she was obliged to her partner for his thoughtfulness in speaking to her on the subject. At this, her partner looked deep into her eyes, an expression of such painful intensity on his face, that, where she had long known him to have a *tendresse* for her, she now realized him to be very deeply affected indeed. She was not surprised therefore at his request for a few moments' private conversation with her, and had not the heart to refuse it, thinking that if, as she suspected, this was to be a declaration, she would at least have the opportunity to convey to him, as kindly as possible, that although valuing his friendship, she could feel nothing more for him.

Accordingly, as soon as it was possible for them to withdraw discreetly, she found herself in a quiet corner of the deserted library, listening with compassion to a heartfelt declaration and offer for her hand. Sir Henry had seemed so self-reliant a man, amusing, a little conceited, fond of feminine company, yet resisting effortlessly for years any attempt to draw him into matrimony, that the scene was even more painful than might have been expected. She refused him in a manner as gentle as her sympathetic nature could devise, and was horrified when he knelt against her skirts, burying his face in their folds. Impulsively, she bent down to stroke the fair springy hair, already a little gray at the temples, attempting to comfort him.

It was at this moment some atavistic sense, some instinct, caused her to glance up toward the door. Where before it had been a little ajar, the deserted library being considered sufficient privacy in itself, it was now swung wide open, and framed in its entrance was Mr. De Brandon, a look of such cynical hurt and bitter disappointment on his face as to give her a physical shock. So they remained, the two of them, staring at each other over Sir Henry's unknowing head. That Hugh De Brandon had mistaken the scene before him was apparent: but even as Harriet sought how in some way to inform him of his mistake without further distress to her disappointed lover, he was gone, the doorway again empty.

She did not see him to say goodbye and she realized he must have deliberately avoided her; so that for once she had not the heart to indulge Miss Neligan, during the drive home, with her usual amusing yet unmalicious observations on the company her aunt had sat with that evening. Indeed, the incident had put her quite out of frame, and she was only glad Selina had not accompanied them, being engaged to take dinner at her fiancé's house, and afterward to play at Family Whist; for she did not feel she could have sustained the foolish, artless chatter of Anne's young sister that night. Indeed, pausing only to make sure that Amelia's new gown had been safely delivered to Mount Street, she retired to bed, to pass an unhappy, restless night.

The following day, passing Mr. De Brandon's house on her way to drive in the Park with Anne, she observed the shutters to be already up, and the house to have that indefinable melancholy, deserted air of a dwelling empty and closed for a long period of time. She could not account for the feeling of desolation that assailed her.

CHAPTER VIII

The time dragged by, and no word came from Mr. De Brandon. Harriet, whose hopes had at first been sustained by knowing the dismal delays even special couriers were subject to, was gradually forced to admit to herself that the continued silence could not be ascribed solely to such difficulties ... it must be that Mr. De Brandon had not yet written. And since she knew, instinctively, that whatever frame of mind he had left England in, however mortified or angry with her he might be, he would never go back on his word, or deliberately fail to accomplish what he had promised to do, then the only conclusion could be that matters were very grave indeed, and Mr. De Brandon was experiencing such problems regarding her brother that he had no time, or nothing encouraging as yet, to write about.

This was distressing, and constant reflection on the subject was causing Harriet's looks to fall off again. Her aunt remarked, sometimes caustically, on her continual anxiety for so worthless a brother, but more often bracingly, that brooding would not help; and so together with Selina, a willing ally, she attempted to divert Harriet's thoughts, but with less and less success. Harriet *tried* to smile, attended the usual social activities that Miss Neligan and Selina constantly chivvied her to, but her heart was not in them, and the strain of appearing to be so for her aunt's sake began seriously to tell. To make matters worse, the Keithleys were still from London, Edward Keithley's estate matters proving considerably more involved than had been expected, and even threatening a lawsuit, and although they constantly begged Harriet to join them in Surrey, she preferred to remain in London, as there, she felt, she would hear earlier, and possibly more fully, should any news of Geoffrey arrive.

She was leaning one evening, in just such distress of spirit, on the balcony of Captain Hartley's handsome house in Berkeley Square, where Mary Hartley, more artistic than her soldier husband, was presiding over a musical soirée, when a mood of almost unendurable melancholy flooded over her. The night was warm, indeed, the Season was almost over and the summer upon them, so that the long windows stood wide open onto the Square. Perhaps it was the liquid notes of the harp falling plaintively on the soft, still air, or perhaps the melody, one she had known as a child, affected her; but suddenly the past, the whole tenor of her present life, Geoffrey, Mr. De Brandon, Amelia, even her aunt's advancing years, assailed her. The past so sad, the future seeming suddenly to hold nothing but trouble, uncertainty, and inner loneliness, Harriet's eyes filled with unaccustomed tears, and trying to prevent these spilling over by staring hard at the fretwork of lacy leaves and spindly branches against the domed sky, she was unware that someone had joined her until Sir Henry Bohun's hand fell lightly on her arm, and he said in his deep pleasant voice, "Alone again, and so worried?"

Harriet kept her head averted, thinking only to avoid discovery of her tears, but it seemed Sir Henry must be aware of them for he continued gently, "I cannot bear to see you in such distress! You were always wont to be so tranquil, so *composed* ... believe me, nothing that happens to your brother should so affect *your* happiness. He is no longer in your charge; he has chosen his way of life; and no one can hold you responsible for whatever scandal he involves himself in!"

Harriet still said nothing, and her companion went on after a pause, in a low, almost diffident voice, "I know this carries little weight with you; that, unselfish as you are, your *sole* concern is for your brother, and not with malicious gossip. But, my dear, you must not let that concern ruin your life, or cause such anxiety for your welfare among those you love—your aunt, your young friend Miss Selina, or the Keithleys, if they were here. . . . That is not fair to yourself, or others!"

This reproof, however gentle, had the salutary effect of making Harriet a little nettled, and she turned her head, intent on giving the speaker a gentle set-down for interference. But the kindness and compassion on the fine features so close to hers could not be denied, and feeling a sudden surge of affection toward her comforter, as well as realizing the truth of his criticism, she smiled through her tears, and declared she could not think what she was about to behave so miserably. " 'A real glum pot!' as Geoffrey was wont to say when he was younger!"

This was encouraging, and having remained speaking comfortably together for a short space of time until she found herself more composed, the two of them returned quietly to the concert, being fortunate in finding two convenient adjoining chairs during a pause in the recital.

After this episode, Harriet began to see more of Sir Henry. He was kind and pleasant, never forcing his company on her, never expecting her to be other than she was, accepting the moods of silence and depression which still sometimes assailed her, try as she might to dismiss them, with equanimity and never again criticizing her. London was now emptying fast, but Harriet, clinging to her conviction that she would be more like to hear news from Italy in London than in the country, was not anxious to leave; and Selina and Miss Neligan agreeing with her, as well as the Keithleys, who anyway wished to indulge her, she decided to remain until the very end. At this, Sir Henry settled to stay in Town too, so that, with fewer of the *ton* about, and fewer entertainments, especially grandiose ones, to attend, Harriet and he were thrown together a great deal more, and had more opportunity to indulge their common artistic tastes at the play, or the opera, or even at the museum in Montague House. Those concerned for Harriet, Anne and Edward Keithley in particular, when they heard of it in Surrey, viewed this state of affairs with satisfaction: Edward Keithley had been acquainted with Henry Bohun for some years, and recognized him as a kind, intelligent man of substantial means: indeed, a highly suitable companion for Harriet. As for Harriet herself, she knew what she was about: she was more tranquil with Sir Henry and therefore happier;

he was kind, reliable, and predictable; he had a superior mind; almost, indeed, he seemed a second Lord Frome. She felt she could rest again, and although worries about Geoffrey continued to assail her, she no longer felt her emotions to be constantly torn.

But there are always gossips to cause needless distress and this precious peace of mind was cruelly overset within a very short time. Miss Neligan being a little indisposed one morning, Harriet had driven to the Circulating Library on Bond Street to change her book for her, when she chanced to find herself alongside an acquaintance, a pleasant enough young woman, who invited her to walk back with her to her home, but a few steps round the corner on Brook Street. Harriet willingly agreed to this proposal: the day was sunny, yet not too hot, Miss Neligan, she knew, but halfway through her present novel, and she herself feeling in need of pleasant company and a change of surroundings. Having finished their business at the Library, therefore, they turned toward Brook Street, Harriet handing her volumes to the Keithleys' coachman and telling him to drive back to Park Lane, explain that she was gone with Miss Bennett, and then return to Brook Street for her within an hour.

They had just settled themselves in the small salon, however, pleasantly occupied with the new edition of the *Ladies' Magazine*, which had come out but yesterday, when a smart carriage drove up to the door, and two ladies descended. Miss Bennett, glancing through the bay window, said, with no great enthusiasm, "I knew how it would be. Here are the Langlands come to call. We had best bid farewell to our quiet hour together!"

Harriet knew the Misses Langland slightly and felt she could not but concur with Miss Bennett's remark: they were chatterboxes, with no real thoughts in their pretty, well-groomed heads, and though in no way deliberately malicious, yet by their very mindlessness, and the weakness of their comprehension, more dangerous. For they literally *knew* not when their gossip was harmful, everything that entered their heads, whether fact or rumor, immediately being repeated again automatically. Listening for nigh on a quarter of an hour to their artless prattle, interspersed with confidences and *on-dits*, Harriet wondered how they could be as popular as they undoubtedly were with the other sex. One could not, she felt, even gaze at them in admiration for long, because the endless stream of feckless conversation would intrude, and the ceaseless movement of their pretty mouths begin to carry an almost gruesome fascination. So intrigued was she with this train of thought that the prattle washed over her unregarded, until she was brought up short by Eleanor, the younger sister, lisping brightly, "His half-sister is quite Gothic, you know, a latter-day Mary Wollstonecroft Godwin type of female, only not nearly so pretty, who mostly *never* goes into Society, but spends her time in homespun, sitting in a cottage, meditating on the Rights of Women! Indeed it would not at all surprise me to hear she still wore *bas bleus*!"

"And she is come to *Town*?" asked Miss Bennett, for once, it seemed, intrigued by her feather-brained friends' news.

"Indeed, *yes*! And she cannot even do *that* properly— why, the Season is well nigh over!—but she is here, sitting at home with our mamma, this very minute!"

"No, that she is *not*," answered Miss Bennett, "for she is but now stepping down from your mamma's carriage outside the house!"

All eyes turned to the window again: and there indeed, descending from the imposing Town carriage, heavy with its armorial bearings, was the Misses Langland's mamma, the Dowager Lady Weston, followed by a strange angular female in unrelieved black, with an old-fashioned hideous bonnet. The salon party waited, listening in silence to the ring of the bell, the heavy tread of a footman, and the muffled conversation in which the butler's heavier tones could be heard saying deprecatingly that Mrs. Bennet was from home, but her daughter was sitting with friends in the salon, if her ladyship would be pleased to step that way. There was more conversation, in which Harriet thought with surprise to hear her own name, and then in no time at all, the door opened, and the newcomers were upon them.

Greetings were brief, for the stranger, obviously with little time for any formalities, asked bluntly, "Which of you is Lady Frome?"

"Why, I am," replied Harriet, too amazed to resent the rather hectoring tone in which the question had been asked.

"Then I must beg you to desist from involving my half-brother in your affairs. He has," the newcomer added, lifting her hand imperiously to forbid any interruption, "enough unpleasant, indeed one might almost say *nefarious* or *unsavory*, affairs of his own to keep him wholly occupied!"

Harriet experienced a series of emotions, but cold fury triumphed. She said, spacing her words, and with such disdain as to rivet all eyes upon her, "If you will do me the courtesy of giving me your name, and that of your half-brother, I might, Madam, be better able to comprehend you!" But even as she spoke, she suspected what the answer to her question would be.

"Hoity-toity!" declared this unpleasing parody of a woman, and then brusquely, "As to who I am, I am Maria De Brandon. But *you* will not know *me* as I have no time for the foolish antics of Society. My brother, however, you cannot deny knowing. He is Hugh De Brandon."

Harriet felt a *frisson* of apprehension. But she said, striving for calm, and in deliberate, reasonable tones, that she had no intention of denying this friendship, but would only point out to Miss De Brandon that *she* was involving herself in Harriet's affairs with neither excuse nor reason.

"Reason! I have reason enough! Here is my friend Professor Ciano come from Rome with unwholesome tales of that profligate Roman Society which have reached the ears even of the academics! *Your* brother, Madam, has caused a scandal that involves one of the oldest aristocratic houses, and as a consequence of your interference, *mine* has had to *crawl*, to lobby for favors, to pay off a duelist, and go surety for a knave to the tune of thousands of pounds!"

Overcome, Harriet could only stammer, "And my brother—how does he go on? Is—is all well now?"

Miss De Brandon snorted, "I could not say, nor do I care. I heard he was sick, but whether there is any truth in this, and whether sick from a wound or jail-fever, I know not!" She pushed her harsh hatchet-face directly at Harriet. "I have had nothing to do with Hugh for years . . . but I am still concerned for our family name, *my* name, as one of the Liberators of Womankind, and this kind of scandal will spoil all. . . . Is it not enough," she continued, in a hot, searing voice, patently unable to stop herself, "that he kills—yes, I say *kills,* for he killed her as surely as if he had taken a weapon to her—his wife? And sullies our name with his profligacies? Without adding the antics of another such fool to his own disgraces!"

Here, at last, she stopped. The company, stunned by both her news and her invective, was unable to speak, Harriet in addition a prey to fear in that her brother might even now be seriously ill or worse. She overcame such weakness, however, with her usual good sense, for vain imaginings would help no one, and turning to Lady Weston as the most reasonable and eldest of the company, asked with some diffidence if she might have the use of her carriage to convey her quickly home since her own was not yet returned.

"For I feel I must be doing something! Yet what, I do not know: I am unable to comprehend what has happened. Indeed, I have heard nothing from Mr. De Brandon since his departure."

Lady Weston proved to be a woman of both good sense and sensibility. Taking Harriet's arm, she said kindly that she would, of course, drive past Mr. Keithley's on her way to her own house. Then pausing only to commit Miss De Brandon firmly and without argument into the care of her daughters, to travel home with them in their carriage, she turned toward the door saying, "My coachman already knows your direction," and adding in a low voice, as soon as they were out of earshot, "Indeed, we are but come from Mr. Keithley's: I was forced to take my unpleasant friend—one from my schooldays, I should add—to his address since Maria had already ascertained that that was where you were to be found, and nothing would stay her!"

This kindness from a near stranger almost overset Harriet, but swallowing hard, she thanked Lady Weston, and trying to put from her mind the wide-eyed and speculative stare of the Misses Langland, and the concerned expression on Miss Bennett's pretty face, she climbed into the carriage with her deliverer.

It was with almost hysterical relief that, on arrival at their destination, she saw Edward Keithley's traveling coach at the door, having obviously but that instant arrived. Pausing only to ask Lady Weston if she would not step inside for a little time, which her ladyship tactfully declined to do, Harriet hurried into the house, and came upon Anne and Edward Keithley, still clad for outdoors, in the library. That something untoward had happened could not be missed: Edward was standing by the fireplace with a letter in his hand, and Anne, on Harriet's precipitous entry, ran over to her, saying gently, "Oh, I am so glad you are arrived home! This very morning Edward received a letter directed to Surrey from Mr. De Brandon, and we are come here at once to tell you—"

Here she paused, and taking Harriet's unresisting arm, settled her into a chair, explaining, "It is both good, and bad, my dear. Geoffrey was in bad straits, it is true, when Mr. De Brandon arrived. The Count D'Antiglione, whose wife Geoffrey so rashly courted, is very powerful, and through him Geoffrey was held in prison for debt, on some foolish technicality. It seems in a wild game of hazard, he had wagered some family stones of considerable value, and having lost the wager, because he could not hand these over at once, was committed to jail incommunicado, thus preventing him from making any arrangements to have the jewelry brought from England!"

She looked at Harriet's dazed face, the lines of anxiety across her brow, and added, as to a child, "It was all prearranged, you understand, the impromptu wager, his gaming companion, everything, by the Count. He *wanted* him to—suffer—there, because he had stolen his wife's affections and made him a laughing stock in Roman Society. They are positively medieval in some respects in Italy, you know! But it seems Mr. De Brandon spoke to the right people, and himself attended on the Count to obtain Geoffrey's release, so *that* is resolved!"

"And the duel that I heard spoken of?" asked Harriet faintly, knowing from Anne's worried air that the bad news was still to come.

"Mr. De Brandon writes that that was the Count's first attempt at retribution—a picked quarrel with an ace duelist. But that bubble was pricked, firstly by Geoffrey's Roman friends, and then by Mr. De Brandon himself ... I fear with money ... when attempts were made to revive the quarrel."

There was a pause, until Harriet said slowly, "Then why are you looking at me with such concern?"

Anne glanced up at her husband, who, coming forward at once, explained with great gentleness that Hugh De Brandon wrote Geoffrey to be ill of a fever, having contracted a putrid sore throat when in prison, and this, because of his predicament and total isolation from his friends, turned later to an inflammation of the lungs.

"But that was some time past; Mr. De Brandon's letter was written nigh on ten days ago, so he may well be recovered by now."

"Let us at least hope he is well nursed," said Harriet somberly.

Glancing keenly down at the emotionally exhausted woman before him, Edward Keithley suggested a glass of wine would do no one any harm, and the three of them were very soon seated more comfortably, better able to discuss the situation. Never one to entertain morbid thoughts, or deliberately to provoke them, Harriet soon rallied, telling herself firmly that Mr. De Brandon would undoubtedly have Geoffrey's recovery in hand, indeed that it was likely her brother was by now near recovered, and Anne fostered this view, reminding her of Geoffrey's strong constitution, which never seemed to fail him. After this, as Harriet would seem to have regained her composure, Mr. Keithley announced his intention of sending a letter of inquiry by messenger next day, and acceded to Harriet's urgent entreaty that if they received no further news within the shortest possible time, he would himself set off with her to Italy, since where she could not help resolve her brother's affairs, she might well be of use in nursing him should this prove necessary. The conversation then turned to less serious yet nevertheless galling apects of the affair, Harriet telling them of Miss De Brandon's recent invective and adding that the story would be all over Town and in the Provinces too, in no time, since the Misses Langland already had word of it. She observed that, to her mind, gossips were of all people the most uncharitable, forever blackening, whether by malice or foolishness, people often harmless or misunderstood, as well as those who better merited such treatment.

At this, Edward Keithley gave her a long look, and said with some embarrassment, "Harriet, I would not wish to give you further pain, but while we are speaking on this subject, my dear, and of Miss De Brandon's criticism of *her* brother, as well as your own, I—I think you should know there is some truth, not just villification, in what she says." He hesitated, then went on carefully. "I know the *warmth* of your nature so well . . . and we are all agreed that Mr. De Brandon has done his utmost to help you and Geoffrey in this affair. . . . Moreover, I, as well as others, cannot fail to have observed your apparent liking for him before his departure. But he is a man I should not myself wish to become well acquainted with—"

"Why?" asked Harriet bleakly, remembering again, despite herself, Mr. De Brandon's strange fascination: his cold arrogance and his sudden disarming confidences, his apparent imperviousness to people's feelings and his sudden, repentant sensitivity, his seeming indifference to his daughter changing to sudden concern.

Edward Keithley replied evenly, "There is no doubt, I repeat, *no doubt*, that his wife left his house at night after some altercation earlier in the evening; and killed herself by losing her footing on the coast path that leads to the main highway. That is the charitable interpretation. Your gossips whisper, of course, that she *ran* from the house in despair, and *jumped*. Neither interpretation can ever be proved. But the altercation can be vouched for: the servants, many of them old and trusted, and including the housekeeper, who is a good, superior sort of woman, had to admit to the Magistrate under oath to hearing the quarrel . . . and also to Mr. De Brandon's frequent impatience and bad temper toward his wife."

"I wonder," said Harriet fiercely, knowing it to be a childish observation, and attempting to ignore the unexpected shock and pain these indisputable facts had caused her, "that they do not say he *pushed* her and have done with it!"

Edward Keithley answered dispassionately, "He was all the evening and well into the night at a bachelor friend's house, a Justice of the Peace, playing chess. The housekeeper was in the salon with Elizabeth De Brandon when he left his own home . . . and his wife's body was found in the early hours while he was still with his friend, by a night fisherman who saw something unusual on the rocks, and sailed as near as he dared to investigate."

There seemed little more to be said. On Harriet's inquiring how Mr. Keithley had learned all this, he replied quite frankly that he had made it his business to inquire, since he had heard something of the story from the Bentleys before their departure from his house some two months ago, George Bentley, on reflection, being a little disturbed to have introduced such a dark horse into Mr. Keithley's household. Edward Keithley had, it seemed, ignored this at the time, but later on noticing the increasing friendship between Harriet and Mr. De Brandon, had become a little concerned and begun his inquiries.

"Yet you allowed this man of—doubtful—reputation to execute a commission for me of the greatest importance and difficulty—and in so doing put us both under an obligation to him!" She added, "It would seem, anyway, that he was good enough to undertake such a responsibility, though not to accept as a friend!"

Edward Keithley's dark countenace flushed, and he said abruptly, "There was little else I could do: he was, so obviously, the only man who could help your brother. . . . If you must know, at our last meeting—for he called again on me on his way to catch the Dover packet—I was made aware he had discerned my earlier hesitation in asking for his help, and realized its cause, for he took deliberate care to introduce his past history into our conversation, and tell me about his wife's fall to her death . . . he also took care to let me know, in a devious fashion, that I need have no fear that *your* feelings were in any way involved with him; that your heart was undoubtedly elsewhere."

Harriet, her mind in turmoil, could say nothing, and Edward Keithley continued. "I believed him; indeed, I *liked* the man despite everything, and felt that since he was eager to help and no threat to your happiness (which is both Anne's and my concern, my dear), he should be left in peace to his own conscience." He added, in a kindly, encouraging tone, "And indeed, he was right about your feelings for Sir Henry, was he not?"

Harriet did not answer directly, but said, "Does Henry know Mr. De Brandon's history?"

Anne forestalled her husband's reply to this question, saying in her gentle voice, "Yes, he, too, knew the story. He was already afraid for you before he knew you so well, yet could not lightly bring himself to further damage a man with a reputation already in question. He *tried* to warn you, but felt he had only partially succeeded, and so came instead to me, knowing us as dear friends, to warn me of Mr. De Brandon's history for your sake. Only, of course, we already knew it."

At this picture of Sir Henry, so universally kind, so concerned for her, yet so chary of damaging another's good name, Harriet's heart warmed toward him. Mr. De Brandon's character was dubious, his integrity in one matter at least, doubtful. . . . Sir Henry, on the other hand, was all that was good, honest, and reliable. Edward

Keithley, narrowly watching Harriet's thoughts chase across her transparent countenance, felt a great relief of mind: there was indeed no danger from Mr. De Brandon, and all was set fair for Henry.

CHAPTER IX

Poor Harriet, her world was once again in a turmoil. Added to her greatest, her constant worry, her concern for Geoffrey, she must now face the truth about Mr. De Brandon; yet, despite her deep affection, indeed something more than affection, for Sir Henry, she could not quite drive from her mind the image of Hugh De Brandon she had earlier held, of a man of strong, passionate character, misunderstood and therefore maligned. She chided herself for a foolish romantic: all those whose judgment and opinion she most valued had no doubts as to the truth of the matter; indeed there *were* no doubts, and it was irrefutable that Mr. De Brandon had, by his cruelty, caused his wife's death. Arrived at this conclusion, Harriet nevertheless found herself seeking excuses for him, until, quite out of patience with herself, she set out alone the following morning for a brisk walk. If asked whither she was going, she decided, she would say to Miss Bennett's; if she met no one, she would merely turn about after walking a sufficient distance and return again to the house, for she had no wish, if the truth be told, to talk with anyone, merely to walk her thoughts away.

This was not to be: she had gone but a short distance from Park Lane when she heard her name spoken, and looked round to see Jane Bentley smiling down at her from a light tilbury. With Harriet, courtesy, and a sense of behavior, invariably overruled inclination, however determined she should be that *next time* this should not be so. She stopped; exchanged news of acquaintances; discussed the weather; and found herself, finally, alongside Jane Bentley in the tilbury, having been unable to refuse a very pressing invitation to meet Jane's mother, who was but now arrived in Town from Bath.

Mrs. Laxton proved to be a comfortable woman, of far greater charity, Harriet suspected, than her daughter. She received Harriet kindly, and began an unexceptionable conversation in which no gossip, and little curiosity except that of natural kindliness, were to be found. Harriet was just congratulating herself on having found the best relief possible for her tormented mind when, once again, the door bell rang and visitors were announced. This was in fact in no way surprising as it was the hour for morning visits, yet Harriet could not help feeling bitterly that it was invariably her fate in life to run into chattering gossips when she least wanted to meet them. When she saw who the visitors were, moreover, her spirits sank still further: the formidable Mrs. Wentworth, accompanied by a gentle inoffensive creature some years her senior, who was found to be her unmarried sister-in-law, and the Misses

Langland with their mamma Lady Weston, who was also, it seemed, a friend of Jane's mother. In vain Harriet wished she had not decided to walk that morning; or if so, had settled to visit Miss Bennett; it was too late now to repine. All that was needed, she decided grimly, was the inimical eccentric Miss De Brandon to complete her discomfort. But this visitor, at least, she was spared, as it seemed that Miss De Brandon had returned to her strange house in the Lakes, with her natural foods, her herbal medicines, her social tracts, and her, to say the least, unusual friends, who admitted to nothing in common save their exceptional minds, so much further enlightened, they felt, than everyone else's.

The conversation turning, perhaps not surprisingly, to this Eccentric, Harriet for once found herself in accord with Mrs. Wentworth, who opined Miss De Brandon to be a most unpleasing woman, with no social behavior, and indeed, with nothing at all to recommend her. The reason for this dire criticism soon became obvious when Mrs. Wentworth described a scathing verbal attack she had sustained, in her own withdrawing room, concerning all she held dear—balls, routs, the "Marriage Market" (here Mrs. Wentworth shuddered), even Almack's and its doyens. Indeed, she finished indignantly, she had been forced to listen speechless to the dreadful creature's tirade, taken, as she had been, completely by surprise. Harriet had to suppress a smile at the thought of Mrs. Wentworth laboring for once *speechless* with astonishment, but was soon restored to a more serious frame of mind by Mrs. Wentworth's next topic of conversation, which was, inevitably, Miss De Brandon's brother. With a glance of hidden malice at Harriet, she began to rake over the story of Elizabeth De Brandon's untimely death, putting the worst construction possible on the affair, "as we are all friends here and can therefore speak freely!" At this, Mrs. Laxton made some attempt to interfere, but was too easy a person to succeed against a woman of Mrs. Wentworth's caliber; and when Lady Weston also intervened to more avail, she had the ground cut from under her feet by her hostess herself, who, ignoring alike both her mother's mild protests and Lady Weston's marked disapproval, at once trotted out the story of Hugh De Brandon's calling on her husband George, who was an old school friend, and whom he had not met for many years, and of his subsequent revelations. The entire conversation took place so fast that the harm was done before it could be stopped, and Harriet, torn between her obligations to Mr. De Brandon and her certain knowledge of his culpability over his wife, trembled between a spirited defense and discreet silence. At this point she saw the wide, avid eyes of the Misses Langland upon her, and in addition to her very real gratitude to Mr. De Brandon, her natural sense of justice, coupled with a dislike of underhanded gossip, prompted her to speak out in his defense. She could not, she said, pass judgment on his family affairs having, in common she suspected with everyone present, no first-hand knowledge of his household at that time, but she did not hold with condemning a man behind his back, and moreover, as Lady Weston and her daughters, at least, knew, she herself had reason to be grateful to Mr. De Brandon for the help he had given her brother. The effect of this speech, delivered with deliberate composure, was to produce an utter silence. Looking calmly round the circle of faces, she marked the Misses Langland's eyes to be rounder than ever, Mrs. Wentworth's smilingly full of malice, Jane Bentley's excited and speculative; only poor

Mrs. Laxton looked distressed at what she felt to be a social blunder of some magnitude which would be all over
Town within a day, while Lady Weston regarded her with
a kind of concerned approval that Harriet might, in other
circumstances, have found amusing. It was the last who
took the situation firmly in hand, and with a quelling look
at her daughters, and a glance of some distaste at Mrs.
Wentworth, said lightly that there were many sides to every question, and what a fine Season it had been in the
main. This deliberate banality had the required effect, and
the ladies were soon on far safer and more conventional
ground, remembering recent social occasions, and gossiping, some of them, with only slight malice about absent
acquaintances.

As soon as she could, Harriet rose to go, explaining
that she had been afoot when she had encountered Jane
Bentley, and must therefore start for home soon, since
Miss Neligan tended to worry these days if she were overlong abroad without saying where she was bound. Refusing the offer of a place in their carriage from various
ladies, she took a rather cold farewell of her hostess and
Mrs. Wentworth, an indifferent one of the Misses Langland, and a considerably more cordial one of the two
older ladies. As she left the room, she could feel the
changed atmosphere, and was aware of the chatter that
would ensue, despite Lady Weston's disapproval and Mrs.
Laxton's distress. It was not a pleasant sensation, and
throughout the walk home, she did not cease chiding herself for so laying herself open to further gossip. She had
given a completely wrong impression of her feelings by
her defense of Mr. De Brandon, she had done Mr. De
Brandon himself no good; indeed, she had inexplicably

thrown away the sophistication of many years for little, or no, reason.

It was inevitable that, rehearsing such thoughts in her mind, she reached home in great perturbation of spirit so that Anne, meeting her as she hastened to the privacy of her bedchamber, asked her what was amiss. Attempting to pass the matter off with her usual apparent indifference and an amusing comment, she suddenly found herself unable to speak, her throat taut with emotion, and her eyes filling with tears. It was too much, the shock and strain concerning Geoffrey, the unavoidable truth about Mr. De Brandon, the sensation of being stared at, and spoken of, as if a freak, with such a brother and such a friend. She allowed Anne to escort her to her room and then gave way to what she felt to be shameful tears. Anne, who had been used always to considering Harriet as not only older, but far stronger in character, more emotionally balanced, and less sensitive than herself, was quite horrified. And waiting only to overcome Harriet's feeble remonstrances and get her to at least rest on the chaise longue, she went in search of her husband to discuss what was best to be done. Edward Keithley, concerned also at such a breakdown in Harriet's seemingly indomitable spirit, was strong in suggesting an immediate withdrawal from Town, and a week of peace and quiet in the country. This more especially as he had now promised Harriet that if no further word of Geoffrey arrived within a week, she should go with him to Rome to ascertain what had happened. For such a journey, and its dubious outcome, she must be rested; moreover, it was likely that Hugh De Brandon would write, as he had previously, direct to Surrey, and anyway a responsible servant could be left in Town to post down at once if any word was received in London instead. With all this in mind, Mr. Keithley put his suggestion of an immediate return to Surrey to Harriet later in the day when she was a little recovered from her distress, and with her usual good sense she agreed, saying only that she must see Sir Henry before her departure to explain her reason for leaving so suddenly.

Within two days therefore, taking just their personal belongings with them and leaving the servants to close the house in Park Lane, the party left London and traveled down to Surrey, Selina only choosing to remain with her fiancé's parents for a further week, when she would return to her sister's as company for Anne should Edward Keithley and Harriet be obliged to travel to Rome. Harriet herself and her aunt were persuaded to go directly to the Keithleys' house in Surrey, Miss Neligan stating frankly to Anne that she was relieved not to have to return to Dorking and have sole care of Harriet in her niece's present state of mind. This state was deceptive: never one to cause others concern, Harriet succeeded in hiding most of the time the almost unbearable worries that assailed her, but that she suffered beneath the calm exterior, all her friends knew, and they viewed her pale looks, and occasional distraught air, with dismay. Sir Henry Bohun had followed them discreetly but a day later, and living as he did in the vicinity of the Keithleys, was unobtrusively helpful in soothing and diverting Harriet's mind. She was grateful for this: and each day that passed revealed further his excellent qualities of tact, sympathy, and general warmth of heart.

It was but a day before their departure for Italy, all having been arranged by Edward Keithley to involve the minimum of fuss, and Harriet's boxes being already packed and strapped, when something occurred to upset all their plans. Harriet, uneasy, eager like all expectant travelers to be on her way, had wandered out into the garden. Behind her, through the open windows of the library, she could hear Edward Keithley giving final instructions to his steward, while to her left, away toward the stables, someone was attempting to calm a spirited mare, and the shouts of the grooms could be clearly heard. She walked on, through the garden, and into the park beyond, the voices fading as she drew away from them. In the park, the sun dazzled down through the trees, the soft air murmured with all the sounds of early summer, and Harriet's memories of other summer days, at her grandparents' home, at Frome Hall, at Knoll House, with Geoffrey first as a gentle child, then a gay companion, invariably charming and pleasant to be with, even later during his many escapades, assailed her.

She sank sadly down on a fallen log in a little copse, so occupied with the past, with unhappy thoughts and vain regrets, that she was unaware of anyone approaching until some ripple of movement disturbed her deep absorption. She looked up suddenly, and there before her, tall, completely at ease, his blond hair afire in a shaft of sunlight slanting through the trees, was Geoffrey himself, smiling down at her, his eyes both mischievous and gentle. In that first instant, she was like to faint from shock, but this passed, and rising to her feet, she hurried toward him, asking how he came to be there, and how he did, and all the questions which rushed into her delighted and astonished mind. Geoffrey laughed affectionately, took her hands firmly, and said encouragingly, in his lazy voice, that she must steady up a bit, he would not suddenly disappear like an Arab djin, and if she would but be patient she should hear his entire history ... but *after* he had eaten, as he was like to die of hunger, having posted from the coast that very day. Even in the delirious relief of seeing him safe and in good health, it occurred to Harriet that she was once again falling into the role of foolishly anxious sister, while he appeared the competent, unimpeachable brother, master of his destiny yet tolerant of his sister's unnecessary fears. She knew she should rather have asked him how he came to arrive unannounced, and taken him to task for his behavior in Rome and of the trouble and concern it had caused. But her delight and relief were so great that she pushed this thought away, resolving to speak so another time, and together they walked back to the house, Geoffrey talking gaily and unconcernedly of nothing, as though he had but come from the neighboring market town, and been away but a few uneventful hours instead of many anxious months. Regarding him narrowly as they returned, however, Harriet remarked that, close up, he had aged considerably. Perhaps his time in prison and his subsequent sickness had taken their toll, for there were tiny, tired lines round his eyes, his nose was fleshier, his skin doughy and rather sallow beneath its tan, the eyes themselves lacked luster and were world-weary: at last, she thought sadly, Geoffrey's seemingly eternal, ebullient youth was fading, and he would soon, if he continued his present mode of life, become that pathetic creature, the *jejeune*, the aging charmer.

Her thoughts were stopped abruptly, however, on arriving at the house and coming upon Mr. Keithley as he left the library: after his initial surprise, he shook Geoffrey's hand gravely, asked him with some reserve how he did, and commented on his sudden arrival in such level tones

as to convey implicit reproach. Harriet fell silent, hearing
in retrospect her foolish, delighted chatter as she entered
the house: that Edward Keithley was pleased to see Geoffrey returned safe and sound could not be denied: but that
he had various questions to put to him, and would welcome some explanation for his scandalous behavior, and
for causing his sister and others so much concern and
trouble, was indisputable. Geoffrey, his eyes suddenly
veiled, remarked this, but said smoothly, with easy charm,
that he was devilish tired and hungry, and if Edward would
but take him to greet Anne, he would then eat, sleep, and
be available for discussion later. He succeeded in convey-
ing by his manner, that Edward had no right whatever to
demand anything of him, whether an explanation of his
conduct or an apology to his sister, but that he would
humor him, all the same, as an old friend.

Edward, knowing he had indeed no jurisdiction over
Geoffrey, took him, with his most saturnine look, to pay
his respects to a very astonished Anne, and afterward left
him to his meal and his rest. Then, having already ascertained that all Geoffrey's luggage was following close behind in the care of his man, and sent a groom to attend to
Geoffrey's mare, which was still grazing just off the drive
through the home park, where he had tied the animal on
seeing his sister a little further away within the grounds,
Edward hurriedly sought Harriet, finding her in the salon.

Alone together, the two old friends looked at each
other in silence, until Harriet said, with seeming inconse-
quence, "But Edward, I am so *very* glad he is home . . . I
have suffered such tortures thinking of all that might by
now have befallen him!" At this, her voice quavered
despite herself, thus causing Mr. Keithley to remark,

dryly, that they should have known her brother would fall on his feet, and they had been, both of them, foolish beyond belief to worry so much. He then added, more to himself than to his companion, "But why *Brighton?* How comes he to have arrived *there?* The nearest port for the Continental packet is Folkestone. . . ."

Here he desisted, for it was suddenly apparent to both of them that Geoffrey had not come directly back to Surrey; and seeing the pain in Harriet's eyes, Edward regretted having spoken, wishing she had been able to retain a little longer her unadulterated happiness at her brother's return. He attempted to divert her thoughts by discussing what must be done to cancel their Italian expedition, however, and within a reasonably short space of time Geoffrey was again sitting with them, graciously prepared, with conscious charm and wit, to speak of his experiences in Rome and his subsequent voyage home to England.

There was nothing new in the Roman story, which was in all respects as Mr. De Brandon had already described. Geoffrey, however, perhaps naturally, presented himself in the best light, and forebore, out of courtesy he said for her sex, to speak in much detail. Harriet for once found herself a little sickened by his speciousness, and thought he had his story, and his answers, too pat by far. She inquired deliberately, as soon as she might, of Mr. De Brandon's part in the affair, and was told, with an easy laugh, that he had been *useful,* but this was said in such a manner as to imply that Geoffrey himself had, in fact, matters completely in hand, and that Hugh De Brandon's efforts had merely hastened the solution a little. That Edward Keithley did not for a moment believe this tale was obvious from his expression, and Harriet herself felt she knew

Mr. De Brandon well enough to be certain he would never *pretend* to having done more than he actually had. She felt mortified for Geoffrey's foolish conceit and lack of generosity in not acknowledging Mr. De Brandon's help, and this feeling was not lessened by her brother adding, again with his facile laugh, that Hugh De Brandon must certainly be *éprise* of Harriet's *beaux yeux* since he was a cynical, selfish fellow who had never been known to do anyone a good turn without some sort of anticipated reward in his life.

"And the way he worked, opened his purse, intrigued like a Machiavelli, even begged and toad-ate that revengeful old Count D'Antiglione," concluded Geoffrey, thus rebutting his earlier claim to having had the solution to his difficulties in his own hands, "could only mean one thing: he was fond of our family. And as he certainly made it obvious he couldn't stomach *me,* well, that left *you,* Sister, as the object of his chivalry!"

This vulgar and complacent speech being unanswerable, Harriet was reflecting sadly that it was not only Geoffrey's features which had coarsened suddenly, since he had used, even quite recently, to be a person of a fastidious and sensitive turn of mind, when the door opened to admit Anne and Miss Neligan. Geoffrey rose gallantly to escort them to their chairs, but Miss Neligan bridled at his approach and voiced, with her sometimes unfortunate forthrightness, the question that had been in everyone's mind, yet remained unspoken because of concern for Harriet's feelings or, in Harriet's own case, a desire to protect Geoffrey himself.

"I bid you good afternoon, Geoffrey. You have, as usual, caused your sister great distress, and had the world in an uproar! I tell you frankly I am not interested in the devious in's and out's of such a sordid affair ... but I wish you will explain to me what you were doing but now in Brighton, as I collect it is *not* a port for the packet boat!"

If this was said deliberately to provoke, it succeeded in its object. A slow, heavy flush spread over Geoffrey's cheeks, and he said, a little thickly, that he had had business of long standing with a friend there, and being within reasonably easy ride of Brighton when he docked, had broken his journey to Surrey to spend a couple of days there.

"*Petticoat* business, I'll be bound," guessed his formidable aunt, with the freedom of expression of an earlier, more outspoken generation.

It was evident, from the surprised, suspicious, and then furious expression on Geoffrey's face that Miss Neligan had hit the mark, and realizing this, she burst out, in unaffectedly astonished, outraged tones, "That you could do so! And poor Harriet nigh out of her mind with grief and worry!"

Harriet put out her hand to stop the exchange, which she felt to be painful in the extreme, and Geoffrey, muttering something unintelligible, flung away toward the window. But as he moved, he swayed a little, and Harriet then realized how thin he was, and wasted with illness. His bright, ready smile, his shining blond hair, his whole manner, had previously hid this, but now, with his ebullient charm and his physical attributes dimmed, it could not be missed. Of a sudden, his jauntiness seemed no longer offensive, but pathetic; she said his name with quick pity, and was rewarded with the defenseless, bemused, appealing regard of a far younger Geoffrey. Edward Keithley, looking on with resignation, knew Harriet to be once again lost, lost in her utter absorption in her brother's affairs. He glanced at Anne, who answered him with a speaking look and together they left the room, taking a rather unwilling Miss Neligan with them.

CHAPTER X

Harriet did not completely divulge what had passed between her and Geoffrey when they were alone, only explaining when she rejoined the others that her brother would seem to be well nigh exhausted mentally as well as physically, and for once, she hoped, really repentant of his actions. This had been said so often before that it carried little weight with the Keithleys, and still less with Miss Neligan, but noting Harriet's drawn features and air of utter weariness, they said nothing. Harriet had not finished, however, and it was less resignedly, and with something like dismay, they heard her continue.

"He admits to Mr. De Brandon having helped him beyond the bounds of common kindness; and says in his gratitude he offered to call in on his little daughter and her governess in Lancashire . . . since he intends to pass

in that direction on his way to Lord Grafton's house in
Cumberland, where he had long ago arranged to stay after his return from Italy."

This sentence was so loaded with uncomfortable possi-
bilities that Anne looked up quickly, and Miss Neligan attempted to speak, but with a curious gesture of command
and ruthless resignation, Harriet went on.

"He cannot remain here: Selina is due to arrive tomorrow, and I know we are all agreed that such a reunion is
not to be advised for some time to come . . . for *her* sake
especially. If he returns to Knoll House, he is too close to
his former friends for their social comfort as well as his
own: he could, if his stay in Italy had been an uncep-
tionable one as we had hoped, have returned and picked
up the thread of his life in the country again. But it was
not: and we all know that the story of his excesses and
their result is already the *on-dit* in London, and fast circulating elsewhere, too."

She fell silent, and it was left to Edward Keithley to
say, gently, "What exactly are you proposing, Harriet?"

She flashed him a look in which gratitude and apprehension were mingled, and explained, "I feel he would do
better in the North, for many reasons of which you are
aware: and Lord Grafton, you may remember, is a reasonably steady young man with a sensible wife. As for his
promise to take in Mr. De Brandon's *en route,* you know
Geoffrey's flashes of selfless generosity,"—she gave a wan
smile—"and I am convinced this was one of them, since
he knew the child's age and physical health when he offered, and now, of course, has been made acquainted by
me with her history. . . . He spoke to me very earnestly of
such an action being a small return for a very great
kindness."

Here again Harriet paused, looked down at her hands, and finished. "Besides, there can be no danger of anything going amiss with the entire plan. He . . . he has persuaded me to accompany him, as *a safeguard,* he says himself, *for his own behavior* during his stay at Lord Grafton's."

This was greeted with utter consternation. Miss Neligan asked whether Harriet realized what she was committing herself to, and how long the visit to Lord Grafton would last: Anne remarked gently, but in a very worried tone, on the tiring journey and the heavy responsibility; Edward Keithley merely said flatly, "And Sir Henry Bohun? Before you absent yourself for what will certainly be some length of time, I think you will agree you owe some thought for him."

An appeal for someone's convenience other than her own could never fail to affect Harriet, and she replied with less assurance, "I am not *committed* in any way to him, you know, Edward. I am extremely fond of him, and I know his feelings toward me. But for that very reason, perhaps it would be best for me to go away for a little, to be *sure*, you understand, that I reciprocate those feelings."

This was so patently an improvised loophole that Edward Keithley's countenance darkened and he looked his scorn. Harriet said placatingly, "I must see him before I leave, of course . . . I shall drive over early tomorrow and explain."

"And he is so besotted, he will doubtless agree; and so carefully conventional, never propose to accompany you!" thought Edward. But he knew Harriet when her mind was made up, and said nothing.

Indeed, everyone realized matters to be settled, and that it would be useless to attempt to prevail on Harriet, her brother now her sole concern, to alter them. Poor Miss Neligan again tried to insist on accompanying her, but was laughed kindly to scorn by her niece, and told that a brother, a personal maid, Geoffrey's valet, and two coachmen should be sufficient escort for even the weakest and most timid of females.

The rest of the day was fully occupied, therefore, with packing, to be certain of being away on the morrow in the early forenoon, before Selina's arrival, with her future parents-in-law and her fiancé, later the same day. Geoffrey, having not yet unpacked his boxes, was free to arrange all matters pertaining to the journey, having, it transpired, already, on his arrival in England, sent word to Lord and Lady Grafton of his pending arrival, and insisting to Harriet that the house was so vast, and its owners so fond of company, that the addition of a sister would hardly be noticed. Normally, Harriet would have demurred at this casual attitude, but matters were so pressing, with gossip about Geoffrey rife, and Selina almost upon them, that with all her former ruthlessness where Geoffrey's convenience was concerned, she agreed to let the present arrangement stand.

Her hurried visit to Sir Henry Bohun was, she admitted to herself, distressing. He had not proved as easily amenable as she had supposed, his love and concern for her causing him to put all kinds of objections in her way, and to speak very strongly on the selfishness and unreliability of her brother. This, however, was an unfortunate move on his part, for it gave her the opportunity to be angry with him in defense of Geoffrey; and powerless, like all men in the face of determinedly devious female argument, he found himself drawn into a controversy about Geoffrey himself, instead of about whether Harriet should accompany him north or not. He thus lost the argument: by the time he had calmed Harriet's anger, soothed her, and lovingly reinstated himself with her, it was already assumed by both that she should go. Having won her way, Harriet felt sorry for him, and exceedingly fond of him; an hour of tender conversation followed, at the end of which Harriet reflected unhappily that she had far rather remain in Surrey, with Sir Henry to comfort and sustain her. But this, she knew, she could not do: she must not fail Geoffrey who, after such a terrible ordeal, would surely this time, and with her help, endeavor to mend his ways. So she said her sad farewells to Sir Henry, and the next day to her aunt and her dear friends Anne and Edward, and set off northward with her brother, their luggage following close behind in another conveyance, in the care of her abigail, Geoffrey's man, and the second coachman.

CHAPTER XI

Geoffrey, having admitted to feeling rather weak and not quite the thing, had been prevailed upon to travel in, instead of alongside, the carriage, so that brother and sister were of necessity thrown into constant conversation with each other on their journey. Both tried to avoid any reference to Italy, Geoffrey affecting a debonair manner, which he soon gave up under his sister's gently understanding glance, and Harriet herself talking rather feverishly of the past Season and similar harmless matters. But such safe topics were no proof against their inner thoughts, and eventually Geoffrey said, awkwardly, that he had almost forgot, he had been asked by Mr. De Brandon to give his regards to his sister. Harriet, who without acknowledging it to herself, had hoped for some such message in the letter to Edward, as a sign she had been at least forgiven that last misunderstood meeting in Sir Henry Bohun's library, was mildly pleased to receive this. But her precarious sense of comfortable content was shattered when Geoffrey added moodily that he supposed he had better tell her that Mr. De Brandon had undoubtedly expected him to reach home earlier than he in fact had, as he had said he would not write again, this time with news of Geoffrey's release and happy recovery, since Geoffrey would arrive far faster than any letter, and be received with far greater joy. On hearing this, Harriet's heart sank as she contemplated her graceless brother: *knowing* there to be no letter of good news, he had even so taken his time journeying home. Indeed, she now suspected him to have halted elsewhere besides Brighton, but she did not inquire, telling herself that at least he had owned to delaying his return, and that that must suffice.

This dismal reminder of Geoffrey's fecklessness and lack of concern for other people's feelings, however, caused further restraint between them, so that they took some refreshment at one inn while the horses were being attended to, and ate their dinner and retired to bed at another, in almost total silence. Harriet, waking next morning to a wet, windy summer's day, felt hard put to continue the journey, Edward's taciturn disapproval and Sir Henry's deep and loving concern recurring constantly to her mind. She imagined Anne, and Miss Neligan, too (for she had been persuaded to remain at the Keithleys' during Harriet's absence), going about their pleasant daily tasks thinking anxiously of her own progress, and she finally descended to the private parlor they had commanded in no very amenable frame of mind. This was not improved by Geoffrey not appearing until a good half-hour after the time appointed for breakfast, and grumbling that he would as lief be safe in bed at Knoll House. She held her temper and her tongue, however, and had the satisfaction of arriving that evening within fifteen miles of Mr. De Brandon's house, tolerably rested.

It had been agreed between them that they should arise late the following morning, and make their way comfortably to Hoyton Hall, arriving suitably about noon. Amelia would by then, they reasoned, have finished her lessons, and her governess be more easily available for conversation. They could talk to the child, do all that was proper, and leave in good time to get well on their way toward Keswick before nightfall, in readiness for the last part of their journey in Cumberland. Harriet, looking forward with mixed feelings to seeing Amelia again and talking with her governess, intended to stop in the small market town of Ulverston on their way to Hoyton Hall, hoping to find some childish treasure, a box made of seashells, or a pretty netted purse, perhaps, to brighten Amelia's life a little.

Having rested well, and the morning, although at present somber with early mists, promising to be fair, Geoffrey was in far better spirits and looks than on the previous day. They were successful, too, in finding a gift for Amelia in Ulverston, and leaving the main highway some little distance past the town, followed a winding lane through a more low-lying, wooded area. They had already been told by the landlord that they would come upon Hoyton Hall suddenly, on emerging from the woods, and as it was large and quite unmistakable, should have no difficulty in following the remainder of the route. This proved to be so, but Harriet was not prepared for the wild and gloomy picture which met her eyes: Hoyton Hall had been built some seventy or so years earlier, in Strawberry

Hill Gothic, high above the wooded plain: it towered there, its lacey turrets, its formidable battlements, its grim central tower, rising above the tall old trees that grew up the hill slope. The damp morning mist, so frequent in that part of the world, and not yet dispersed, trailed ghostly fingers across the long facade, so that everything, terraces, stone steps, dark windows, looked to her as if they might vanish away like an evil dream in a fairy tale. Geoffrey, seated beside her, must have been similarly affected, for he grunted and observed that no wonder the poor little monster was sickly in body and possibly mind, if she had to live in that grim pile! They drove on through the tall heavily heraldic lodge gates, left open and apparently unattended, and along a reasonably kept drive, the long gray edifice seeming to tower further and further over them as they approached it. The last part of the drive, however, rose sharply, and after two quick turns, they found themselves outside the wide stone steps leading to a heavy studded door.

They had ridden in the cumbersome coach which had carried maid, valet, and luggage north, having left their own carriage back at the inn, since they had been warned of the bad state of the country lanes, which could ruin a light traveling carriage built for the greater speed of the main highways. The dark, enclosed, ungainly vehicle seemed so in keeping with the vast, unwieldy size of the house before them that Geoffrey could not help but laugh, saying they were come, anyway, in a suitably Gothic fashion themselves, and blended well with their surroundings. A hollow jangling bell reducing him to a state of almost uncontrollable mirth, they waited with the gleeful anticipation of two schoolchildren for the door to open. But here all resemblance to Ann Radcliffe's fearful romances ended abruptly: a smart young footman, impeccably uniformed, opened the door, received them very correctly, and showing them into a salon which, if over-heavily furnished, was yet dustless and shining and without a cobweb or spider in sight, said he would inform the housekeeper of their arrival, Miss Amelia and her governess being at present walking in the grounds. The housekeeper, too, when she arrived, could have appeared to advantage in a far less remote part of the world, and obviously performed her duties as scrupulously in the absence of her employer as when he should be in residence. Ringing for refreshment for the visitors, she explained that Miss Phipps and her charge were expected to return within a very short while, if they would be pleased to wait, and then herself withdrew. Harriet would have liked to ask her how the child did, and secretly hoped to glean some unwitting revelation about the house and its family, but the housekeeper had been so formally correct and distant in manner that this was quite impossible.

Geoffrey, having by now recovered from his mirth, remarked that *within* the house at least, all seemed comfortably unexceptionable, and perhaps it was, after all, the child's fault, not her surroundings, that she suffered her various spasms. She might, he opined, be just spoiled, or plain evil-tempered, like many pampered children who saw little of their parents; or, indeed, like some who saw a great deal of their mammas! Remembering Amelia, her manner and her general behavior, Harriet was sure that this was not so, but as there seemed no point in such speculations, she said nothing, merely waiting in companionable silence with her brother for the return of the walkers. . . . The house was, all the same, very silent, she realized, almost smotheringly so; on one side of the room, the trees grew close to the window, and the mist, not yet dispersed, curled silently among the branches, clammy and depressing. Harriet turned her eyes quickly to the summer log fire, thinking that perhaps the heavy comfort could not quite dispel the sense of isolation and somewhat inimical nature. Geoffrey must have been having similar thoughts, for strolling toward the long windows overlooking the terrace and formal garden beyond, where flowers and shrubs hung sadly in the damp air, he said casually, "A glimmer of sunshine would be no bad thing, all the same! And I'd as lief spend the *winter* elsewhere."

He had hardly finished speaking when the door opened with no previous sound of voices or footsteps, indeed with no warning at all, and Amelia stood with Miss Phipps in the doorway. They had already removed their cloaks and bonnets, and changed their pattens or boots for pumps, Amelia's fine hair had been newly brushed, too, all of which indicated their having been within doors for some little time, unheard. It was ridiculous, Harriet told herself, to expect therefore to have detected a childish voice, or running feet, or *some* spontaneous reaction to the arrival of visitors: for all she knew, the pair might have entered by a far door or the nursery be situated in another part of the house, thus explaining the lack of any childish sounds. But in some fashion Harriet felt this not to be so; that even if the door they had entered by had been very close, and the nursery adjoining, the same stillness would have obtained. Even as the thought flashed through her mind, however, she acknowledged Miss Phipps pleasantly, and put out her hand to the slowly advancing child, saying warmly, "Good morning, Amelia! Here are my brother and I come to pay you a visit on our way further north still!"

She was rewarded with a very faint, shy smile, whereupon Geoffrey, who unexpectedly had a way with children, though he seldom exerted himself to use it, solemnly extended his hand too. This was taken, after a short pause, very formally, revealing that Amelia, guarded and reserved though she might be, had nevertheless beautiful manners, and everyone sat down to talk a little. But Geoffrey, obviously quickly bored by the stilted conversation that ensued, constantly jumped up and walked round the room, peering at the display niches, even poking into a cherry-wood needle workbox, half hidden in a corner. At last he turned with the appearance of having firmly made up his mind, and announcing his intention of taking a short stroll, asked if Amelia had done her walking for today, or whether she could accompany him. But at this, the child looked first apprehensive, and then unwilling, and her governess's murmured encouragement producing an expression near to tears, Harriet intervened and suggested Amelia show her her room and the nursery-cum-schoolroom instead, adding that she had a little package somewhere in her reticule for her young hostess. This was agreed to, although Amelia's smoke-gray guarded eyes showed little enthusiasm, and Geoffrey setting off alone on his walk, Miss Phipps left her young charge in Harriet's hands.

They went at a sober pace up the wide carpeted staircase, with its massive wrought-iron railing, to the rather dim corridors of the first floor. Amelia flitted down these like a little ghost, looking neither right nor left, and eventually, at the end of a particularly long wide passage, hesitated, glancing longingly, it would seem, upward at a short spiral stair, but apparently feeling she was expected to continue straight on. Looking ahead, Harriet could discern a handsome gallery, with long recessed windows the length of one side, and many portraits adorning the other: she glanced inquiringly as the child, who said, in a subdued voice, "That is the Long Gallery; it is said to be very fine."

The stilted adult phrase, obviously picked up from her elders, amused Harriet, and she asked, encouragingly, "And do *you* find it so?"

"No," replied Amelia, in a tense little voice, "I *hate* it!"

This was so unexpected that Harriet was momentarily at a loss, but she recovered quickly, saying matter-of-factly, "Then we shan't bother with it. This looks an intriguing little stair—shall we go up there instead?"

The child's face brightened, and she replied, with something very like warmth in her voice, "Yes! This is my very own stair, now. . . . *You* are thin enough to go up it, but Miss Phipps is *not,* so she goes always round through the gallery, and I come this way."

The last part of this sentence came out with a rush, almost as though Amelia did not wish even to speak of the gallery, and had unwittingly been led to do so in her spontaneous enthusiasm for her little spiral stair. Harriet wisely forebore to ask the reason for this intense dislike, and they climbed in a more companionable silence until, arrived at the top, they crossed a narrower, less luxurious corridor to enter the nursery-schoolroom. This at least, Harriet was pleased to see, was light, white-painted, with large windows overlooking the home park. The walls were adorned with two suitably chosen engravings by William Say, with a few samplers rather laboriously worked, and here and there, with colorful daubs of flowers and animals, very creditably done by Amelia herself. As well as color and movement, there was an inner life in them, a sympathy in the simple rendering of a furry ear, or a soft nose poking through grass, as though the lonely little girl felt inarticulately akin to the shy, wild creatures; whereas there was no attempt to draw people at all. Harriet allowed herself to be taken sedately over to a table where shells gathered, it seemed, near the Estuary, were laid out prettily in boxes, and pressed flowers displayed in a large looseleaf book. These treasures reminded Harriet of her own gift, a puppet doll, and producing it, she said gently that she hoped Amelia would like it, as it was just such a present as *she* had loved when she was eight years old. Amelia was obviously enchanted with it, and, for the first time behaved like any other little girl with a gift—she danced the strings, walked around it, patted it, sat it in a place of honor over the mantel, and could not thank Harriet enough for it. At last, however, she left it, and in greater amity than ever before—except perhaps when they had visited the animals at Astley's—she walked her grown-up guest through an arch into her bedroom. Here, the clothes closet still stood open, the only sign of Amelia and Miss Phipps having hurried in order to greet their visitors. The clothes hanging therein were certainly plentiful, but mostly so drab in color, so drearily *serviceable,* with no feminine frills or tucks or ribbons, that Harriet's heart smote her. There was however, one brighter splash of color there, one pretty gown: the dress made from the material they had bought on Bond Street some time ago. But this hung pinned in soft paper and protected by an old scarf-shawl, quite unused. Two pairs of eyes surveyed it, and Amelia, fingering it, said apologetically, "I do like it, Ma'am, but I have no chance to wear it here," and at this, the half-realized, half-formed idea which had lain at the back of Harriet's mind took hold. It would seem foolish to spend such a very short time with Amelia, since she now seemed so much closer to accepting Harriet's friendship, as Mr. De Brandon had at first hoped. Perhaps, therefore, she and Geoffrey might stay overnight at Hoyton Hall (for their change of plan should present no problem to so competent a housekeeper), and Amelia might be permitted to dine formally with them this evening, in her best gown. And on the morrow, too, they could take the child on an expedition to Cartmel Priory, or to the Estuary for a breath of fresh air, returning early in the afternoon so that they could continue their own journey in good time. The more she revolved the idea in her mind, the better it seemed, for apart from giving Amelia a small treat, and perhaps gaining her confidence sufficiently to discover a little of what so troubled her, Harriet would have a better opportunity to talk with Miss Phipps, to hear how things had gone recently with the child, and even perhaps to air the matter of Amelia's fear of the Long Gallery. Accordingly, she said nothing to the child, but later approached Geoffrey after his walk, and having secured his easy, good-natured agreement to the plan, spoke first to Miss Phipps and then to the housekeeper, with satisfactory results.

Harriet's opportunity to talk informally yet at some length with Miss Phipps presented itself later that afternoon; she had been walking on the terrace with Amelia and her governess, a party to a pleasant nature lesson which Miss Phipps was giving her pupil, and, the lesson finished, Miss Phipps suggested Amelia go to her room to rest for a little, since she would be up far later than usual that evening. Amelia having left in her usual quiet and docile fashion, Harriet determined to begin her discussion with the governess at once, and asking if she could spare a little time to talk of Amelia, gestured her to a stone seat nearby, and sat down beside her. Miss Phipps, knowing Harriet to be seriously interested in the child, and the recipient of Mr. De Brandon's confidences about her, was only too ready to talk for, as she explained, the fact of Mr. De Brandon being absent overseas and therefore inaccessible worried her. Amelia had not, it seemed, much improved, being as silent and uncommunicative as possible and, indeed, seeming sometimes a little recluse, in not wishing to walk about the grounds even. She had not, it was true, suffered one of her strange, hysterical fits for some time, but on the other hand, her nightmares and sleepwalking were, Miss Phipps felt, increasing: as though the falling off in the hysterical fits had caused her to suffer more in this other respect.

As soon as she might, Harriet asked if the governess had noticed the child's fear of the Long Gallery.

"I have indeed, Lady Frome, many times, and am at a loss to explain it! She has always been so, and I can only conclude it to have something to do with—well, with her mother, perhaps? For Mr. De Brandon told me long ago that as a young child she used to play happily there, rolling her soft ball on wet days, or playing hide-go-seek with her mother. She was always, I understand, very much indulged in those days."

This was said with a hint of kindly disapproval, but was followed almost at once by her continuing very concernedly, "And that is *another* thing, my Lady! She seems now to avoid *other* places, besides the gallery. There's the park—she won't walk near the wall adjoining the rose garden; indeed, it has been difficult to get her that side of the house at all, since her nightmares started! Oh, it is all so confusing and *worrying!*"

Harriet herself, feeling extremely disturbed, ventured to suggest that these places, too, like the gallery, might have some association with her mother in the child's mind, but this was so uncomfortable an idea, since she was obviously so afraid of them, that Harriet suggested instead that perhaps the child was frightened of some*one* rather than some*place*. "But how can that be, Lady Frome? There is no one here she does not know, and the servants are all invariably kind to her. . . . No, I would say myself that in her nightmares she sees those places, and so becomes afraid of them in her waking hours!"

This was a possible explanation, though Harriet was not happy with it, feeling that it begged the question, in that the nightmares themselves remained unexplained even if the child's fear of certain places was accounted for. She had hoped for better news of Amelia's progress, and felt unaccountably cast down in consequence. However, turning her mind to more practical matters, she made a point of asking Miss Phipps herself to be present at dinner that evening. "For it would be bad, I feel, for her to put you and me in separate worlds, Miss Phipps. I mean," she added hastily, suddenly realizing this might be interpreted as a social distinction, "for her to associate my brother and myself with a normal outside world, and you with her, of necessity, more closed life here, with all its memories and possible fears."

Miss Phipps might be a somewhat uninspired companion for a child, but she was intelligent: she twinkled a little, and said comfortably that she quite agreed with Lady Frome, and would be pleased to dine with them. "I shall even dress myself up a little, so that the affair will seem more festive!"

A servant having already been dispatched with word to

Harriet's maid and Geoffrey's man of their employers' intention to stay overnight at Hoyton Hall, and instructions to pack accordingly a small valise each with necessities, including a dinner gown for Harriet and similar attire for Geoffrey, it had already been agreed, with the housekeeper's connivance, that the dinner would be as gay as possible an affair; and Harriet was touched that Miss Phipps, too, should so fall in with their plans.

As for her suggestion of an outing for Amelia the following day, she was pleased to find the governess welcomed this, too, with enthusiasm. After this having nothing of importance left to talk about, they fell comfortably into a discussion on every child's need for companions of near their own age, Miss Phipps, it seemed, being one of six children, three of them very close in years, who had lived happily together in a small parsonage, their father being curate of a large but poor parish. So the time was whiled away pleasantly enough, until the dressing gong sounded, whereupon Miss Phipps hurried away to attend to her own and her little charge's toilette.

CHAPTER XII

The dinner party the previous evening had been a great success, Amelia pleasing everyone by showing signs of real animation and, even when silent, seeming to be happily content. That this was partly due to Geoffrey, Harriet had no doubt: he would seem, she thought wryly, to have a way with even the youngest of females, giving them his complete attention, and making the recipient feel he considered her the most fascinating and interesting person he had ever met. Under this wholly kind and gentle treatment, Amelia almost sparkled; the gray eyes lost their wary expression, and no longer downcast, she gazed at her new friend with open innocence. There was, too, a kind of rapprochement between the two: without in the least condescending, her brother seemed to sense a child's thoughts and feelings; perhaps his lonely and misunderstood childhood with his father had given him this intuitive sympathy. Only once, indeed, did he falter, when attempting to tease Amelia for her stubborn refusal to walk in the grounds with him the previous day; then the thin little face lost every trace of expression, the eyes fell again, and a closed look ensued, quite startling in its contrast to her previous open regard. Never disconcerted for long, however, Geoffrey rallied, and said in tones of mock misery, which were yet made effective by carrying a hint of real resentment, "Well, I see I have not, after all, made a real friend of you yet, or you would never answer me in such a fashion!"

At this the child looked up quickly, and flashing him a glance of anxious appeal, said awkwardly. "Oh, no, you *must not* feel that way! It is just that—that I do not choose to walk in parts of the garden,"—she glanced round the table, sensing the question in every adult mind, and hurried on, but to Geoffrey alone—"I had used to—to see my mother there sometimes, and—and my father—and I cannot . . ."

Here the small voice faltered again and Geoffrey, sensing the child would say no more, and sorry for her distress, broke in lightly, "Oh, I was but quizzing you, Amelia! It is of no great consequence, for I know, really, that we are already fast friends!"

Amelia cast him a grateful look, but remained silent and withdrawn again for some time after, it taking all Geoffrey's determination and charm to revive her spirits.

The next day, riding comfortably in the large old coach, with Amelia once again in good heart and the sun shining in a cloudless sky, Harriet felt them to have achieved a great measure of success with the child. Her behavior was still a little quaint, old-fashioned, and restrained, in that she sat so docile, never even asking to poke her head out of the open window to feel the breeze on her cheeks, or demanding when they would be arrived at the sea; but since it was obvious that she was happy and content as she was, this signified little.

They had decided on the sea in preference to Cartmel Priory or Ulverston, considering this to be a more exciting expedition than a visit to a ruin, or a stroll round some little shops and a visit to a small museum, the only interests these places had to offer. Amelia was gratifyingly excited, and when the housekeeper produced a large picnic hamper, her delight increased. Harriet was a little put out, admittedly, by being told, low-voiced, by Miss Phipps, that Amelia's father had earlier made similar efforts with no such happy results, but she put this information to the back of her mind, to be considered at a more suitable time, and attended to the matter at hand.

Once they arrived at their destination, the rest of the morning passed pleasantly, Geoffrey first of all showing Amelia how to skim stones into the sea, a somewhat unladylike pursuit which Harriet turned a blind eye to since there was no one to observe them and the child was so enjoying herself; and then searching the rock pools for shells or tiny fish. After all this activity he lounged comfortably against one such rock, his beaver over his nose to Amelia's amusement, while she and Harriet, seated more decorously on a flat stone slab covered with the carriage rug, laid out the picnic. Alas, all too soon it was time to begin the homeward journey, and ordering the coachman to carry everything up to the carriage, which had stood on the rough road some small distance away, the three travelers decided to walk a little along the cliff before entering the vehicle and turning toward home.

Their walk brought them to a large village, with some rather more superior houses surrounding a pleasant green, and it was at one corner of this, close to the village shop, that Amelia stopped short, gripped Harriet's hand, and then turned blindly, as though to flee. She cannoned into Geoffrey, however, who caught her by the shoulders, saying kindly, "Here, here! Bolting like a young colt! Now, what's the matter?"

Amelia, her head buried in the skirt of his coat, gasped something incoherently, pointing her finger toward a shrubbery adjoining the tall railings of one of the houses, and Geoffrey caught a brief glimpse of a man, tall, well proportioned, his back toward them, bending slightly in some fashion, as though to pick a spray from a tree or greet a smaller person, a child perhaps, but in no way sinister or furtive.

Harriet, too, had seen this, but more clearly, since she was facing the same direction, and undistracted by Amelia's headlong rush, which had caught Geoffrey off balance. Even as both brother and sister gazed, Amelia's head still buried in Geoffrey's coat, the figure straightened up and turned away, having taken, it was revealed, an obviously loving farewell of a small, pretty young woman in a chip straw hat. Stopping to raise his beaver a second time, he then strolled contemplatively off, his back toward them, unaware and careless of any scrutiny. Instinctively, without any discussion, Harriet and Geoffrey followed hurriedly, crossing a corner of the green diagonally, hoping to intercept the stranger near the next corner, and running Amelia between them, her head still averted. They were not quite quick enough to maneuver a meeting face to face, however, so that instead Harriet was forced to turn a little, and almost peer into the countenance of the stranger. She received a mystified and rather affronted stare in return, from a pair of steady brown eyes in an open, extremely normal countenance; and the three of them being now directly in the path of the stranger and hampering his progress, Geoffrey felt constrained to say something, at least, by way of apology, adding that his young friend had thought she recognized him.

On hearing this reasonable explanation, the stranger unbent a little, and smiled down at the top of Amelia's head, albeit a little inquiringly, since her eyes were still hidden. And Harriet said, somewhat sharply, for she was beginning to think the entire incident a hum, "Amelia, child, do you know this gentleman?"

The child peered up fearfully, an expression of relief washing over her features as she saw the stranger's face smiling into hers. She shook her head instantly, and mortified, Harriet made her excuses as best she could, inwardly grateful to the stranger for being so courteous about their waylaying him in such a fashion. Somehow, without further embarrassment on either side, the parties separated, and Geoffrey and his sister returned to the coach with a silent Amelia.

This incident, naturally, put rather a damper on the rest of the expedition, Amelia becoming utterly withdrawn again, and her elders extremely thoughtful. At last Harriet, who felt the day could not be further spoiled than it already was, and that in this case she would be justified in asking a few pertinent questions, said gently, "I wish you will tell me, Amelia, who you thought the gentleman was just now. Did he remind you of someone?"

On receiving the barest of nods from the downcast head, Harriet then asked, even more gently, who it was the stranger had put her in mind of. But here she received no real answer, merely a shake of the head, but whether this was to signify Amelia did not know a name, or would not give one, they had no means of telling. Geoffrey, following his own rather confused train of thought, then asked the child if the stranger resembled anyone she saw in her nightmares, but received such a wild stare of utter panic that he pursued his questions no further.

Arrived home, Harriet told Miss Phipps of the incident, and finding her, as she expected, as confused as herself, suggested the gravity of the situation required her having a word with the housekeeper, since she suspicioned the incident to have something to do with Amelia's earlier childhood, and it transpired the housekeeper was the only upper servant to have been in residence before Mrs. De Brandon's death, even Amelia's nurse having left within the following few months. Accordingly, Mrs. Mason, as she was called, was sent for, and Harriet, recounting the incident at the seaside and expressing herself very concerned about its implications, asked outright if she could throw any light on the matter.

There was a long pause, Mrs. Mason's rather narrow gray face and light-colored steady eyes regarding Harriet impassively, as though weighing her up. At last she said, tonelessly and without emotion, that she had no fault to find with either her employer or his wife, they had both treated her with consideration, and she could tell Lady Frome very little that would be helpful. At this Harriet, concealing her exasperation at what seemed to her deliberate evasion, pointed out that she had asked for neither gossip about, nor any opinion of, Mrs. Mason's employers, merely if she knew of any incident in Amelia's life, either past or present, that could in any way account for the child's general demeanor, or her behavior that morning.

On hearing Harriet's tone of voice, and recognizing tenacity when she saw it, Mrs. Mason looked uncomfortable, spoke about it not being her place to judge, but finally said, still dispassionately, that as for the child's general behavior, Mr. De Brandon was sometimes a violent-tempered man and her mistress a highly emotional woman; that mostly they were discreet in their disagreements, but she had heard, on several occasions, Mrs. De Brandon shouting and crying hysterically, and her husband's voice raised too. . . . Perhaps, she finished, the child had on occasion heard similar arguments; or might, indeed, have witnessed something more violent, which could account for much of her timid reserve, and guarded behavior toward her father.

This matched so well with her own thoughts that Harriet was appalled, but she mastered her emotions, and keeping her face as expressionless as the housekeeper's own, then asked if Mrs. Mason had any explanation for Amelia's more recent nightmares, or her fears of parts of the house and grounds. It was obvious, from Mrs. Mason's oblique and guarded reply, that she associated these dreams and fears, too, with Amelia's memories of her parents' quarrels: any suggestions of strangers wandering in the grounds were firmly denied: the house was isolated and near no town; everyone in the sparsely populated area knew one another and would take note of strangers; and no one living in the vicinity would dream of trespassing or frightening Amelia: Mr. De Brandon was universally well thought of in the district. The morning's incident was therefore quite inexplicable to her.

Harriet was now in a quandary: Geoffrey, tired of his role of kindly uncle, was agitating to be away at once. She had, he reminded her, said one day's delay, to which he had agreed, but longer he could not stomach; the house and its inmates depressed him, and were anyway no concern of theirs.

"You will get no thanks, Harriet," he said, when she told him of her conversation with the housekeeper, "especially as it seems clearer than ever to me that Amelia's father must have a lot on his conscience."

This confirmation of her own views moved Harriet to ask Geoffrey's indulgence at least for the sake of the child, but her brother replied, with his habitual selfish yet clear common sense, "If you are being so melodramatic as to suppose the child to be in any danger from her father, your wits have gone begging, for privately he dotes on her. And if, on the other hand, you imagine *you* can cure her ills, you are even more of a ninnyhammer, since you are nothing to her, all her emotions and maladies being entangled with her parents' affairs. I declare you are become quite mawkish about her, and had best desist at once."

"And what of the curious incident of the stranger today?"

"If you ask me," said Geoffrey bluntly, "the fellow looked somewhat like her father—same tall, broad back, same air—and you can make of *that* what you will. . . . Maybe she saw him embracing her mother, or more likely some light-skirt or other, and it upset her. . . . Or maybe," he added, opening his blue eyes wide with mock fright and grimacing horribly, "he was not *embracing* her mamma at all—rather shaking her, or strangling her, even!"

Harriet knew this to be a foolish and rather sorry joke: Mrs. De Brandon had fallen over a cliff. But the implication of violence throughout the whole affair was not to be denied, and she could not but shudder. Moreover, although perhaps younger, thinner, and less self-assured, she now recognized a similarity between the back of the stranger recently seen and her memory of the commanding figure of Mr. De Brandon, turned away toward the window on the day she first met Amelia.

All this was disturbing, and she tried afresh to persuade Geoffrey to remain a few days longer at Hoyton Hall, but in vain: Geoffrey would not yield. In the event, however, the discussion had finally, as he angrily pointed out, delayed their departure, for it was now too late to leave that afternoon as they had planned, especially since they must first travel by way of the inn they had stayed at two nights ago, to pick up servants, baggage, and the light carriage. With a bad grace, therefore, Geoffrey submitted to remaining one more night, and brother and sister spent an uncomfortable and unsociable evening alone in the salon, quite out of patience with each other. Harriet went up to her room as early as she might, and retired to bed at once, her last waking thought being that if the child seemed no calmer in the morning, she would tell Geoffrey he might travel on if he pleased, but she would remain a little longer at Hoyton Hall to keep an eye on Amelia, Miss Phipps being too kindly unimaginative, and the housekeeper too efficiently impersonal, to be of much help to any child in a crisis.

CHAPTER XIII

For the next few days Harriet did not feel she could leave Hoyton Hall. Geoffrey had long since gone, driving off, as he had threatened, early on the morning following their visit to the sea, and sending the cumbersome traveling coach back to the Hall for her use, along with her maid, her boxes, and the second coachman. Harriet herself, on rising that day, had been approached by a worried Miss Phipps, who said Amelia had passed a very disturbed night, calling out incoherently in her sleep, and tossing and turning ceaselessly.

"My room is across from hers, as you may know, Lady Frome, and I had left my door open because of your account of what had passed yesterday. It was as well I did so, for I am a somewhat heavy sleeper normally, I

confess, and if I had not awakened to comfort her, I am
sure the child would have had an even worse time of it."

She paused agitatedly, and then burst out, "Oh, that
Mr. De Brandon were here! I fear we are due for another
spell of nightmares and night walking, perhaps even hysteria as well, and she will again make herself physically
ill!"

Harriet waited patiently until the governess had talked
herself out, and then said soothingly, though truth to tell
she was herself apprehensive for Amelia's health, that as
for Mr. De Brandon's absence, there was nothing to be
done; but that if Miss Phipps would prefer it, she herself
was prepared to remain for a few days in the hope of
seeing some improvement in Amelia's condition before
leaving to join her brother. The governess welcomed this
proposal with relief, obviously thinking the burden of responsibility to be removed from her shoulders onto those
of the competent Lady Frome.

Harriet, feeling obscurely that she had but exchanged
one worry and responsibility for another (indeed, before
leaving, Geoffrey had remarked petulantly albeit incor-
rectly that Amelia had replaced himself in his sister's affections), now considered best how to proceed. It seemed
of little use at present to talk to Amelia, any question,
however carefully put, throwing her into a sort of fevered
silence that was quite distressing; Harriet therefore attempted, with Miss Phipps' help, to pass the day in an ordinary manner, with some simple lessons; a short airing in
Mr. De Brandon's carriage instead of a walk, Amelia
showing signs of considerable distress when the latter was
proposed; pleasant meals by an open window; and finally,
a simple game of Beggar My Neighbor with Harriet. At
no time during the day was Amelia left alone to brood,

and as she seemed by bedtime a little less tense, wary, and silent, both Harriet and Miss Phipps had hopes of a quiet night. But this was not to be; Harriet, one floor below, but with her door also open, heard the cries, the unintelligible gabbling, the momentary waking as the governess tried to quiet her charge, and eventually went up herself to sit with the child until she fell asleep.

The next day it was obvious that bad dreams had taken their toll; Amelia was unnervingly pale, listless, unable to eat, and utterly silent. She paid no attention to what went on around her, and seemed hardly able to drag herself from the schoolroom to the dining room, or thence to the salon. Miss Phipps prognosticating another hysterical attack of paralysis, Harriet was near despair, and seriously considered sending a messenger to Geoffrey, in the expectation that he knew Hugh De Brandon's direction in Rome, asking him to get word to him that his daughter was again become ill. But this seemed such a tedious business—it would take so long for any such message to reach Rome that by the time of its arrival, the crisis would almost certainly have resolved itself one way or the other—that Harriet decided to wait one, perhaps two, days more. Miss Phipps gave no help in reaching this decision, having ceded authority to Lady Frome, although at the same time assuring her that she would support her ladyship completely in any course of action she might think best to pursue. This having been agreed, the rest of the day was got through somehow, Harriet arranging for Miss Phipps to have one, or perhaps two, nights' complete rest, while she herself sat up for Amelia, though without telling the child of her intention.

Accordingly, that night, after Amelia had fallen into a fitful slumber for some hours, Harriet settled herself, still dressed, on the bed in the governess's room. Lighting the lamp, she attempted to read, but this proved impossible and eventually she quenched it, relying on the soft glow of the night light spilling across the corridor from the child's room opposite. During the past few days the house had seemed more and more close and silent, more depressingly still than ever, and now, in the small hours, with Amelia intermittently muttering and tossing in her uneasy sleep, it seemed to take on a watchful life of its own. It creaked furtively, the branches of the tall tree outside soughed and tapped against the windows, even the governess's comfortable wicker basket chair rustled and clicked as though someone were sitting on it. Harriet, the noises impinging on her consciousness, exacerbating, despite herself, her already raw nerves, thought how grimly such sounds might affect a child, solitary in its own room, and with something disturbing, whatever it might be, on its mind. This observation had scarcely passed through her head when she heard a faint fumbling in the bedchamber opposite, then a small, sinister thump, followed by a strange, slithering noise: Amelia was sleepwalking.

Knowing it to be dangerous to awaken a somnambulist, Harriet rose quickly, and taking time only to light the lamp again and snatch it up, followed the child out into the corridor. Amelia had by this time reached the far end, and was descending, in total darkness, with that same curious sliding yet somehow certain gait, the spiral stair to the next floor. At the bottom she turned without hesitation not away from, but toward, the Long Gallery. Arrived on the threshold, however, she stopped suddenly and began sobbing softly, chattering to herself unintelligibly, yet with such vehemence that Harriet thought she might wake; but she did not, the distraught mutterings died away, and the child continued her strange progress toward the far end of the gallery. Arrived almost at the last window embrasure, however, she stopped once again; then, with an inarticulate cry, scuttled furtively crabwise into the bay before the last one. And by the time Harriet, following with great circumspection, reached her, she was fast asleep, her thin body curled up like a little animal, her head resting on her sticklike wrist. Somehow Harriet contrived to carry the child back to bed without awakening her, and the remainder of the night was spent, with no more nocturnal wanderings certainly, but with a continuous jumbled muttering, the only intelligible words, repeated several times, being "Mamma!" and "Papa!" cried out in an agonized voice, followed by "Oh, no! Do *not*! It is not—" on a note of terrible entreaty.

After such a night, Harriet herself felt drained of energy, and deeply disturbed in mind, not only by the sleepwalking, but by the small snatches of conversation she had heard. She did not speak specifically of these to the governess the next morning, although she would have been hard put to explain why, privately suspicioning the reason to be a kind of misplaced loyalty to Mr. De Brandon, or a last desperate hope that matters were not as they were beginning to seem; she did say, however, that Amelia had cried out the word "Mamma" repeatedly, whereupon Miss Phipps immediately agreed to having heard her do so on other occasions, but never, she added on Harriet's discreetly questioning her further, had she known the child to say anything else, nor had she ever mentioned her papa before.

Harriet, considering Miss Phipps to be too direct, open, and simple a soul to deceive, or behave in such a devious manner as to withhold any knowledge she might have, came to the conclusion that Amelia had, this time, talked more articulately in her sleep than ever before. But she knew not whether this was a good or a bad thing: it might be that such increasing coherence would relieve the child's mind somewhat, and encourage her to speak more openly, in the ordinary way, of what troubled her, but Harriet could not be certain of this, although she spent the day hopefully contemplating the possibility.

If she had anticipated a more restful vigil that night, however, she was destined to disappointment. Firmly advising Miss Phipps that one more period of complete peace and quiet would better prepare the governess to cope with her own vigil the following night, Harriet retired once again to the bedchamber across the passage from Amelia, to read and rest fully dressed, as best she could. At first, to her relief, the child seemed calmer, so that by the early hours she herself was dozing fitfully, half her mind alert for some disturbance that never came. Gradually, therefore, because of the unexpected peace, her own weariness overcame her, and she fell into a deeper sleep, only to start awake a short while later, aware that something was not quite as it should be, that some noise perhaps, or movement, had disturbed her. Once again she lit the lamp, and thrusting her feet into her slippers, hurried across to Amelia's bedchamber, only to find the covers thrown back, and the bed empty. There was no indication of where the child had gone, but deciding hurriedly that like as not she was returned, sleepwalking, to the gallery, Harriet hastened thither as fast as she might.

But the gallery was utterly silent and empty, and Harriet, standing uncertainly in the window embrasure where she had found Amelia before, was about to summon Miss Phipps to help search the house when a movement in the feebly moonlit garden below caught her eye: a small skimpy figure in a dimity nightgown trailed barefoot across the formal garden and into the shrubbery beyond. Harriet whirled, and without pausing to call anyone, ran the length of the gallery, down a side stair, and through the little postern that stood already wide open into the garden. The lonely figure had already vanished, but Harriet took the same direction through the shrubbery, thinking the child could not be far away, since she herself had been moving considerably faster than the little apparition. At the corner of the wall to the rose garden, she came upon Amelia suddenly; indeed, she had barely time to stop herself blundering up the path and awakening her. She managed to arrest her headlong rush in time, however, and stood motionless, trying to control her breathing as the child approached a brick arch that gave onto the rose garden itself. Arrived at the arch, Amelia stepped quite openly through it, only to stop short, gripping the brickwork with both thin hands and staring sightlessly toward the climbing roses that hung festooned from chains strung shoulder-high between decorative pillars. It was then the hairs on the nape of Harriet's neck rose, for Amelia, her head on one side, appeared to be listening intently to someone, then seemed to be on the verge of replying; but instead turned in blind panic, running headlong back along the way she had come, brushing past Harriet and still, it seemed, fast asleep.

Harriet turned again in pursuit, and arriving back at the house, could hear the child's rasping breath as she climbed the stairs ahead, and then utter silence after she reentered the Long Gallery. On reaching this herself, she could at first see no sign of Amelia, but advancing cautiously, she made out, in a shaft of moonlight, the little pointed face peering round the corner of the same embrasure at her; and even as she hurried forward, the thin, tense body, coiled like a spring, hurled itself at her, sobbing hysterically, and with such a depth of relief that Harriet's heart ached for her, "Mamma, oh, *Mamma!*"

It was obvious that, up to that moment, Amelia had still been half asleep, carried along in heaven knows what tormented memory, so that she had taken Harriet's figure, obscurely seen in the dark beyond the shaft of moonlight from the tall windows, to be that of her mother. Now, however, she came fully awake; and an expression terrible in its realization of her mistake, of how matters really were, passed over her face. She began to weep, long racking sobs, but all the same, to Harriet's relief, clinging to her, seemingly for comfort. She lifted the small figure up bodily, therefore, and speaking as soothingly as she might, took her into Miss Phipps' room, and made her comfortable on the blankets and swansdown quilt on the bed. At length the sobs subsided a little, and Harriet, stroking the wispy hair, damp now with exertion and distress, said gently, "Amelia, dearest, I wish you will tell me what frightened you . . . I shall not speak of it to anyone if we agree it should not be told."

This she knew in her heart to mean nothing, for she felt she could persuade the child, ultimately, to speak, if indeed there was anything that should be revealed. But at present for her health, even her sanity's sake, Harriet felt she must be persuaded to share her burden of worry. There was no answer to her appeal, however, so after stroking Amelia's brow in silence for a little, Harriet made another attempt, asking quietly, "Did you surprise your mother—come upon her unexpectedly—in the gallery one day?"

There was the slightest nod of assent.

"And—and was your papa there too?" asked Harriet, dreading to hear the answer. But there was none; no word, no gesture, only a tightening of the child's hand in her own. Her heart sinking finally, Harriet went on, endeavoring to control the tremor in her own voice. "Did something you saw that time distress you?" And then as the tiny nod of assent came again, "*Why* will you never now speak comfortably to your father, Amelia? Did you see him, perhaps, seeming to be unkind to your mamma?"

She was about to add, she knew not why, perhaps to comfort the child, perhaps to exonerate Hugh De Brandon, that there must be some explanation, that Amelia must somehow have mistaken or misinterpreted what she saw, but she had no chance to do so. Amelia leapt from her arms, clear from the bed, and flattening herself against the far wall, cried out fiercely, "It was *not* my father! It was somebody else! He—he was kissing Mamma. And I can *never* tell Papa, because he would be so sad! I saw him crying already when Mamma was dead . . . I expect it was because sometimes he was very cross with her and made her cry . . . but he *loved* her!"

In that moment, some flash of revelation, of clarity, as well as a surge of relief, almost overset Harriet. She asked slowly, staring at the rigid little figure across from her, speaking as though to an adult, aware of the intuitive intelligence of the young mind, "And is that why you never, now, confide in your papa, or accept his affection? Are you afraid that you would have to tell him, that you couldn't help yourself . . . ?"

The child nodded, painful tears running down her face.

"And then—then he would never love Mamma, or me, or anyone, ever again!" At this she began to weep unrestrainedly, deep sobs which Harriet made no attempt to check, thinking it best to let the child cry herself out. But at last the sobs ceased, and a pair of red-rimmed, tired eyes gazed at her from a white, exhausted, and truth to tell, rather dirty face. Watching her narrowly, Harriet decided the immediate crisis was over, but that Amelia was too overwrought to sleep yet; so putting out her hand she suggested they go together to the kitchens to heat some milk on the little spirit lamp Mrs. Mason always kept in readiness there. Without hesitation the child took the hand offered her, and stopping only to wrap a warm robe round the thin body and slip a pair of pumps on the small, still icy feet, Harriet, carrying the light in her other hand, descended with Amelia to the kitchens.

All the time they were dipping the milk from the milk churns in the dairy and warming it, Amelia held her peace, and it was not until she was seated at the scrubbed white table sipping her hot drink that she spoke again. But in doing so she gave Harriet the opening she required, for she asked, timidly, "Was I—was I in the grounds too, Ma'am? . . . Until you tucked them into the quilt, my feet felt so *wet!*"

Harriet replied carefully, anxious to preserve Amelia's precarious calm, "Yes, I found you in the rose garden. You have been there before, my dear, have you not? I collect it is one of the places you dislike to walk in."

For a moment she thought the child would not answer, the closed look appearing again on her face, but then two large tears rolled down her cheeks and she looked up, her expression a strange mixture of sad appeal and fear, to say, "Yes, I—I used to play there sometimes, with

Mamma and Papa, and I—I dream of it, too, you know. Then one day—oh, long after Mamma had died, quite recently in fact—when I went there like I sometimes still did, I saw the man again—" She continued with difficulty. "He—he was standing in the rose garden, and *he* looked sad too, not a bit frightening, so I asked him why he had been kissing Mamma that time. . . ."

"And—?"

Amelia looked up again, her fear now mixed with curiosity. "He—he just asked me how my Mamma did; and when I said she was dead, he—he shook me and asked me what I meant. . . ."

With the memory, Amelia began to sob again. "I tried to get away, but he didn't let go . . . I don't think he *meant* to hurt me really, I think he was so—upset . . . and then he said, as though he was afraid, 'What did she die of?' So I told him she had fallen over a cliff a long time ago, and nobody knew why she was there. . . ."

This time Harriet made no attempt to prompt, but let the silence lengthen, until Amelia finished. "And he said, 'So that's why she never came,' and he let me go, and I ran as fast as I could indoors."

"But you didn't tell anyone."

Amelia said simply, "There was only Miss Phipps . . . and I did not want to speak with *anyone* about the man."

Appreciating the child's half-intuitive, half-reasoned reticence, Harriet passed no comment, thinking that now the reason for Amelia's hysteria and distress was out, the matter was best forgotten, by the child at least. But Amelia had not quite finished. She said thoughtfully, "I had seen the man sometimes before, you know. Before he kissed Mamma, that is, among my papa's friends. But I never knew who he was. . . ."

Disturbed by the brooding expression on Amelia's thin little face, Harriet decided enough was enough; she told her briskly to finish her milk, promising that afterward they would both sleep in Miss Phipps' large bed, just for this one night.

Once in bed, as Harriet had hoped and half expected, Amelia slept deep and dreamlessly. But she herself remained wide awake, a prey to many conflicting emotions, uppermost in her mind being the thought that Hugh De Brandon had both been sadly maligned, and had probably carried an unnecessary burden on his conscience for nigh on two years.

CHAPTER XIV

The following morning both Harriet and Amelia rose late, the one having fallen at last into an uneasy repose, and the other sleeping deep and dreamlessly perhaps for the first time in many months. On waking, Amelia's first request was that Harriet would not speak of anything she had told her to Miss Phipps, and as this accorded well with Harriet's own inclination (indeed, until she had collected her wits and refined a little on the story, she had intended speaking to no one), she agreed at once, merely adding that they must, however, tell her governess that Amelia felt much better, and would probably be quite recovered by the end of the day.

"For she is very kind to you, my dear, and very concerned for you."

Having told Miss Phipps that the child had again

night-walked, but had afterward spoken at last of what troubled her, and that in consequence Harriet had high hopes of a permanent improvement in her health and spirits, she added that she intended to take Amelia for a long drive, both to put some color in her cheeks and to stop her from refining overmuch on her story. Miss Phipps, unimaginative and kindly as she was, evinced no curiosity as to *what* Amelia had spoken of the previous night, merely saying in heartfelt relief, and with her face wreathed in smiles, that she had *known* Lady Frome would, if anyone could, ultimately restore Amelia's happiness and well-being.

The two of them set out, therefore, in an open carriage, for the day was hot and sunny, meaning to be returned for a late nuncheon about noon. Harriet had intended to speak no more that day about Amelia's revelations, feeling that the less important little mysteries and gaps in the story could be explained another time; or indeed not at all, since the bold framework of the tragedy, and the reasons for Amelia's long breakdown in health and spirits, were now apparent. But as they circled the first loop, and continued on down the drive, Amelia pointed to a long vista edged with trees and a small path turning off from it into a glade, saying in a low, but Harriet was pleased to hear perfectly normal, voice, "I saw the man there, too, later still. He said he wanted to talk to me again—about Mamma, you know—but I ran away. . . ."

"And after that you became afraid of the grounds?"

"Yes, I thought he might come back, you see; but he never did. Only, that day at the seaside, you remember? I thought it was *him*."

Amelia's voice had now begun to shake a little again, so saying firmly that they had talked enough about the man, and would soon become dead bores if they were to continue, which made Amelia laugh as she intended it should, Harriet set about discussing more everyday affairs, the visit to London, and how much she could recall of the animals at Astley's, observing with satisfaction that Amelia fell happily in with the conversation, like any normal, intelligent little girl.

They returned about twelve of the clock as they had intended, Amelia pink-cheeked and still talking hard, Harriet laughing, and descending from the carriage, entered by the main door in great good spirits. But once inside some atmosphere, indefinable, perhaps a little ominous, assailed them: and looking up from the child, Harriet saw the tall figure of Hugh De Brandon in the shadows at the back of the hall, his breeches and hessians spattered with mud, and an unreadable expression on his dark, unsmiling face.

He advanced at once into the sunlight falling from the glass cupola of the hall, and said expressionlessly, into the sudden silence his presence had caused, "Good day to you, Lady Frome. What a pleasant surprise to find you here." And then, with hardly a pause, to the governess, who could now be identified hovering in the background, "Miss Phipps, please take Amelia to her room."

Harriet observed he did not greet the child beyond giving her a slight nod, being, it appeared, intent on immediate conversation with Harriet herself. And seeing Amelia drifting away like a little ghost, all her vivacity lost once more, she felt her temper rising. But even as she was about to remonstrate, it came upon her, with awful clarity, how she must look to Mr. De Brandon, living here uninvited, in a house she had never previously visited, instructing his daughter's governess, monopolizing his child, making free with his carriage, and without even the conventional protection of her brother or her aunt to mitigate such unusual behavior. To make matters worse, she was aware of knowing a great deal about his private life which he, it must be presumed, did not: and she had not even come to terms with herself yet, as to whether she should make what she had learned known to him or not.

Accordingly, feeling herself quite overset, able only to stammer a greeting, she allowed herself to be relieved of her bonnet and parasol by a footman, and escorted across the hall to the library by her host. The double doors were closed with a discreet click behind them, and Hugh De Brandon, moving a chair forward for her with what seemed to her frayed nerves an overexquisite courtesy, went to stand before the heavy marble fireplace, its hearth hidden during the warm summer days by a delicately wrought *petit-point* screen. Once there, he said conversationally, yet with his gray eyes dark, unreadable, set unwaveringly on her face, "Miss Phipps tells me you have recently had a great success in saving Amelia from one of her hysterical bouts. I am obliged to you."

This was said in such a manner as to convey the impression that the speaker was anything but obliged, rather, indeed, critical of unwarranted interference, and had the salutary effect, therefore, of jerking Harriet's paralyzed senses into motion again. Remembering her concern and worry of the past few days, her unselfish attempts to help Amelia, and her rejection of Geoffrey's advice as well as his request that she accompany him, she gave Mr. De Brandon a wide stare, and said coolly, "I must apologize for seeming to meddle: I was accompanying my brother, who called here, I understand, because of a promise, or an offer, made to you in Rome . . . and the following day Amelia became so distressed, I—I did not feel I could safely leave her."

"Her—attack—occurred after an encounter during some expedition or other to the sea which you took her on. Or so Miss Phipps informs me."

The implication was not lost on Harriet that such an expedition was harebrained and ill-advised, since it had resulted in such a disaster, and seeing something of her expression, he added languidly, "You need not censure Miss Phipps: *she* is loud in your praises."

Harriet's color rose, and with it her temper. She took a deep breath, however, and said, with controlled iciness, "You mistake me, Sir, I am not censuring *Miss Phipps;* indeed, I consider her a kind and estimable woman!"

There was a heavy pause. Harriet sat with folded hands and firm lips, determined that Mr. De Brandon should make the next move, and having a hard struggle to refrain from saying to his face that everything that had been done had been done with no other motive than kindly concern for Amelia, and at great inconvenience to herself; and that his daughter was now quite likely cured of her strange malady . . . unless, of course, he continued in his cold and distant manner toward the child, in which case he would undoubtedly find himself once again with a hysteric on his hands.

No sooner had she determined *not* to say all this than, horrified, she found herself doing so, finishing, for good measure, and with no remnant of her calm manner remaining, "I did not come here, Mr. De Brandon, out of vulgar curiosity, but on account of my brother's earnest request that I accompany him to Cumberland. Indeed, I would far liefer have remained in Surrey where, as you may remember, I have many friends and much to occupy my time!"

She stopped, appalled at what she might seem to imply, and sensed, without a doubt, the image of Sir Henry Bohun hanging for a moment between them. Hugh De Brandon's face closed, giving him a fleeting but remarkable resemblance to his daughter, but he said imperturbably, "That is exactly why I am somewhat surprised to find you here."

Harriet felt *his* implication to be very clear: that when he had last seen her, she was given every sign of being attached irrevocably to Sir Henry, having earlier misled Mr. De Brandon himself, and later forgot him completely. She recalled in startling detail the scene in Sir Henry's library, and such a confusion of feelings rose within her that she could not speak. Mr. De Brandon, seeing something of an inner turmoil reflected in her features, moved suddenly, and putting out his hand, impulsively said, in a completely changed tone, "Ah, do not let us provoke each other so! Miss Phipps has told me of your devoted concern for Amelia these few days, and I am, indeed, truly grateful. It is just," he added slowly, "that I had known matters between us to be at an end; and although feeling relieved and grateful that Amelia should so have come to trust—nay, if Miss Phipps is accurate, to *love* you—I could not but feel you to have inspired reliance and affection in her only to leave her bereft again, and vulnerable, when you return to your—friends—in Surrey!"

Harriet, knowing this to be the inevitable outcome, could say nothing, only look down at her hands, tight-clasped in her lap, and Mr. De Brandon went on with difficulty, in an even lower voice. "Also I must confess it to have crossed my mind that if you and Geoffrey had not—interfered—to take Amelia out that day, she would never have seen this stranger, whoever he may be, and would thus have avoided at least one recurrence of her malady."

Seeing the expression, once again, in Harriet's eyes, he went on hastily and placatingly, "But I had not then seen the *physical* change, anyway, your presence has wrought in her! Indeed, I must confess to thinking, before you returned with Amelia from your drive, that Miss Phipps eulogic description must be an exaggeration . . . I beg you will forgive me!"

All during the latter part of this speech, Harriet's conscience, too, had been smiting her. This was the man who, thinking her affections already to be fixed elsewhere, and knowing he had nothing to gain, had nevertheless taken endless time and trouble to extricate her brother from his predicament. She was mortified and ashamed, and said, with her habitual impulsive warmth, "Mr. De Brandon, I, too, owe you an apology. I have not even thanked you for all you have done for my brother . . . I cannot"—here she paused, at a loss for words, and ended abruptly—"You have my, my undying gratitude."

He said nothing, merely looked down at her, an expression in his eyes she could not, or dared not, fathom. He seemed to be waiting for her to say more, or about to speak himself, but feeling her thoughts too utterly confused, she could find no words, and he, too, remaining silent, the moment passed: he turned away, remarking levelly that he had been so uncivilized as to forget she had had no refreshment after her long drive with Amelia, and ringing the bell, instructed the servant to prepare a nuncheon for her in the small salon. Then, with a bow, he turned to leave her.

He was already at the door when she recollected Amelia's recent subdued little exit, and wondering at her selfishness in not thinking to speak earlier of it, she jumped up, saying hurriedly, "Mr. De Brandon! You will—I *beg* you will visit Amelia as *soon* as you may! She is very attached to you."

At this, the dark brows rose cynically, causing Harriet to continue, emphatically, "I *know* it!"

Mr. De Brandon studied her in silence, then said in a sardonic tone of voice, "I realize, Lady Frome, that you did not approve of my manner to my daughter just now. But I beg you will collect that I have been avoided by her so many times it has now become second nature for me to be undemonstrative in return . . . especially when I have matters of far greater import to discuss."

"All the same, Sir, you would do well to see her, for I dare vow that this time you will find her changed. If you will but *encourage* her a little!" added Harriet, more urgently, perhaps, than the occasion would seem to warrant.

She received another long look, Mr. De Brandon saying finally, with a reserve that put her quite out of temper with him, "Well, we shall see. I will certainly *try*, although I dare wager that though she will now smile for *you*, she will not for *me*."

It was on the tip of Harriet's impulsive tongue to tell him Amelia's story, for the child's sake if not his own, on the instant. But she could not; she had given Amelia a sort of promise of silence, and must keep faith at least until she spoke to her again. As for Mr. De Brandon himself, she reflected, perhaps Amelia was in the right of it, and he had better never be told.

On his part, Hugh De Brandon stood watching the variety of emotions pass across her sensitive, expressive countenance. He thought, sadly, he had never seen such warmth and intelligence, as well as beauty, in a face, and more to humor her concern than anything else, said as he finally left the library, "If it pleases you, I will look in on Amelia. And we must talk more of her, and of this stranger later, if you please."

He was both amused and intrigued by the apprehensive, speaking look he received in return.

CHAPTER XV

During the afternoon, Amelia being engaged walking in the grounds with Miss Phipps, Harriet summoned her maid to pack her boxes, and the coachman to put all in order for their departure next day, resolving to tell Mr. De Brandon that evening that she was daily expected at Lord Grafton's and request him to be so kind as to lend her a groom for the journey, since she and her abigail would be traveling unattended but for the coachman. She then went along to the schoolroom, where she judged Amelia and Miss Phipps must by now be returned, and finding them there, learned from Amelia that she was expected to spend an hour or so before dinner with her papa as he had, it transpired, brought her some gifts from Rome.

This was encouraging, especially as the child seemed, since her talk with Harriet, to have lost her fear and reserve in speaking at least *of* her father, and appeared, if not happily excited, at least content and at ease. Feeling as though she were abandoning her, yet quite unable to do otherwise, Harriet stayed some time talking, resolving not to break the news of her departure until the following day, in the hope that the child would have a happy evening and a peaceful night, at least. She left the schoolroom at last, however, promising to visit Amelia's bedchamber to say good night before dinner (since it seemed she was not expected by her father to attend that meal), and also to sleep across the corridor from her, in Miss Phipps' room, for one night more.

"And then, you know, Amelia, we must give poor Miss Phipps her room back! It is *most* inconvenient not to have one's things about one!"

As she left them, she was pleased and amused to see both child and governess busily brushing and arranging Amelia's hair, selecting ribbons, and spreading out the pink gown to be sure it had no creases, since Amelia intended to wear it when she went down to her father later.

"For I must look my best, you know, as he told Miss Phipps he came post haste from Rome to see me, thinking to have been delayed too long about his business affairs!"

Harriet herself took some time with her toilette that evening, and the northern night air being cold, damp, and far from summery, went along to say good night to Amelia, looking very handsome in a dark green velvet gown, its tight bodice and sweeping skirt, in the newest fashion, setting off her elegant figure to advantage. She was gratified, albeit amused at herself for being so, by the expression of approval on the faces of both Miss Phipps and Amelia, the child saying that Papa would surely think her very pretty. This made them all laugh, and Harriet settled down to a pleasant, quiet half-hour with Amelia before she should prepare for bed. Aware that the child's problems, and her apparent complete recovery from them, might well be the subject of conversation later in the evening, she said, after they had looked through a book and talked comfortably for about ten minutes, "Amelia, if the matter should arise when I dine with your papa this evening, may I tell him, if I think fit, what you told me yourself last night?"

She added hastily, seeing the expression of doubt and worry which at once clouded the small face, "To be frank, I know not whether I should do so or not; it will depend on how the talk goes, you know. But I promise you I shall only speak if it seems best, and that if I decide to do so, he will *never* be angry with you for it; or with your mamma, my dear."

The measure of trust Harriet had inspired in her young friend was fully revealed when Amelia replied simply, "Very well, if you say so . . . and if it won't make him sad again."

"I shall *only* tell him," said Harriet firmly, "if it makes him *happier*."

Considerably relieved to have passed this hurdle, Harriet descended to the salon before dinner in a rather more tranquil frame of mind, although still undecided whether to speak out about Amelia's discovery or not. That it would come as a shock to Mr. De Brandon she had no doubt, and whether it would be best to say nothing, therefore, or deny any knowledge of who the stranger at the seaside could be, merely letting matters between Amelia and her father take their now presumably happier course unexplained; or to give the reasons for Amelia's strange behavior during the last two years on the assumption that *understanding* of that behavior would guard against any return to it, she could not tell.

She found herself impelled to an immediate decision, however, on discovering, when she entered the salon, Mr. De Brandon already to be there, and obviously awaiting her arrival. He came forward at once, saying with a welcoming smile and an open warmth unusual for him, "You are right, Lady Frome, and I owe you an apology! Amelia greeted me with far less restraint than usual, and was sometimes almost as she had used to be. I know not how you have contrived it"—here his glance fell, with obvious pleasure and approval, on her appearance—"but I feel she will soon be again a lively and affectionate child, as well as vastly improved in looks!"

This was praise indeed, and Harriet said so, taking the opportunity it offered to add that she was relieved to hear such a good report as she could now leave to join Geoffrey at Lord Grafton's with a quiet mind. But this was not well received, Mr. De Brandon objecting that Amelia would not wish her to go, and indeed was not yet sufficiently reestablished to accept her departure without harm to her new-found stability. But Harriet remained firm; she felt it to be impossible for her to stay longer at Hoyton Hall now Mr. De Brandon was returned, she said, not only for propriety's sake, for she suspicioned Mr. De Brandon would laugh this to scorn, but also because she had obligations elsewhere to so many people, her brother, Sir Henry Bohun, and her aunt among them, and must fulfill these as soon as she might, Amelia now being, in her opinion, past the danger of any relapse.

Mr. Brandon greeted this speech, however, with a heavy silence, walking slowly up and down, something very near a scowl on his face. At last, he utterly disarmed her by saying urgently, "All this may be so, but I beg you will remain a little longer . . . I, I—there are things I must ask you about Amelia's previous behavior, things on which Miss Phipps feels sure you could throw at least a little light. And besides, it—it is so long since I have enjoyed your company . . . which I shall not," he added on a low note, "be privileged to enjoy ever again, I collect."

Harriet, in considerable distress of mind, could say nothing. She was committed to Sir Henry, who loved her; she pitied the man now standing with his back toward her, and must soon decide whether to tell him Amelia's story or not; worst of all, she was herself overwrought, and knew not what she wanted, or why. She stood up, struggling to remain calm, to make at least some reply, but was saved by a servant, who knocked, and holding the doors apart, announced that dinner was served. Wordlessly, with a sharp sardonic glance, Mr. De Brandon escorted her in to dine.

Unexpectedly, the meal passed pleasantly enough. There was some constraint at first, but her host had obviously resolved to forget their differences for the moment, and talked so amusingly, yet deferring to her opinion in a way that could not but please, that she was able to regain her composure and respond tolerably well. But on their return to the salon, the tea tray being brought in early and the servants dismissed, the atmosphere became somber once more: Mr. De Brandon, dropping all pretense of a social occasion, walked heavily to the windows, and said in a cold, hard, deliberately dispassionate voice, "If you must be gone tomorrow, Lady Frome, you must. I beg you will forgive me my—importunate appeal—before dinner. But I shall be obliged if you will tell me what has passed between you and Amelia." He then turned and subjected her to the full gaze of his penetrating and now somewhat inimical gaze.

Harriet, feeling her heart lurch with apprehension, was contemplating how best to broach what she must say, and indeed, how much she should divulge. But seemingly he mistook her silence for refusal, or at best reticence, for he barked abruptly, "If you please, Ma'am! At least tell me about this terrifying stranger by the sea: have you reason to know who he was, at least?"

His manner was almost rude, certainly overbearing. Harriet's head came up, and she said icily, deliberately delaying what she feared was the inevitable, "He was a stranger, Sir, whom Amelia had never seen before." And then, aware of the anxiety clouding the angry eyes of the man opposite her, "She—she had mistaken him for someone else, I later discovered."

There was a long, and to Harriet agonizing, pause, until Mr. De Brandon said, very low, "*Who*, Lady Frome?"

She was impelled to ask him, a little unsteadily, although never doubting, in her innermost mind, the answer. "Forgive me, Mr. De Brandon, but when your wife was alive, had you really no idea, no suspicion of—of any *affaire?*"

He looked amazed, but seeing the earnestness of her regard, replied without any of his former dictatorial manner but very soberly, "I assure you, I had, and have, none."

She clasped her hands in her lap, looked down at them, and told him of Amelia's sleepwalking, of the Long Gallery, the rose garden, and, ultimately, of the child's story as she herself had heard it that night, including Amelia's thinking to have seen the man among her father's friends when his wife was still alive. She was aware of the utter immobility of the man before her, and dared not look up, either during the account or when she had finished, her voice dying away in the absolute silence of the room.

So she remained, with her head bent, listening to the crackle of the logs on the summer fire, and the snap as they fell to the hearth, until she was aware that the tall figure standing before her had moved. . . .

He was again by the window, but this time with the heavy drapes drawn back, staring out into the garden, thinking heaven knows what bitter thoughts, his back rigid, the hand that clasped the curtain white at the knuckles. Harriet suddenly pitied him what must be at best his deep disillusion, at worst, something far more heart-rending; she rose quickly, and went to stand behind him, saying uncertainly to his unresponsive back that it was all in the past, that he must not distress himself for, after all, was not now Amelia, at least, cured?

At this, he turned at last, and gazing down at her with an unreadable expression in his gray eyes, said slowly, "You are very good . . . very kind. And you must not concern yourself for me. I had long, I suppose, fallen out of love with Elizabeth; she was my wife, and I strove to make her happy . . . but it became so difficult to do so." His hand dropped from the curtain and he continued, with an abrupt, dismissive gesture, "At first, when I heard you, I felt disbelief; then, perhaps, horror and consternation; but never acute distress. At least, not for myself or Elizabeth: for that poor child, yes, I can imagine how she has suffered!"

He broke off again, and walking back toward the fire, seemingly lost in the turmoil of his own thoughts, went on, apparently at random. "In a way, it is almost a relief. I have been so tortured by remorse . . . I had no patience with her, you know, I never tried to understand her. When I married her, she was so pretty, so gay . . . I knew her to be a little frivolous, without real force of character, but she seemed amenable too, eager to learn, to adapt herself to life in this part of the world."

Harriet, not wishing to hear such revelations, and certain that Mr. De Brandon would later regret having made them, tried to speak, to say she must withdraw, but he appeared not to notice her attempt, only continued in that strange, contemplative fashion.

"I came gradually to understand she would never have any interest in things of the mind, nor in country life or pursuits, or even in what was expected of her among the tenants . . . all she wanted were gay, even wild, parties, and incessant visitors."

He glanced at Harriet, and said bitterly, "Well, I gave her them. I am no Puritan myself, and I enjoyed them. But gradually, the exciting newness of these, and of her life here, began to pall; truth to tell, the county had become a little tired of her extravagances and excesses, and was beginning to avoid us, I suppose. And then she started to hanker incessantly for London . . . even to entice and encourage Amelia, a child not yet six, to demand to be taken there, and become discontented of her life here."

Unable to stop herself, in sudden realization, Harriet said, "So that is why you so objected to Amelia visiting London!"

He replied shortly, "Yes, she had been so ridiculously and wrongly encouraged. . . ." But this matter did not, for the moment, interest him and he went on, pursuing his relentless memories. "Elizabeth became to my mind impossible. Nothing would satisfy her but London, not just for the Season, or any long spell, but forever."

He looked again at her, fiercely this time, and concluded, "But I could not live so. I am a landowner, sometimes absent, certainly, but never permanently so ... I love my land, and I try to be fair and just to my tenants. It was impossible, and so I told her. ... And so began our endless, interminable quarrels with her becoming hysterical, and I myself like a madman with the frustration of it all. ..."

Seeing his distress, at last, fully revealed, Harriet strove to distract him by saying gently, "But for a long time, you were all happy; Amelia too, for at least her mother always loved and cosseted her."

At this, he replied bitterly, "You are an incorrigible optimist, Lady Frome. Elizabeth only indulged the child when it suited her. I admit it usually did, but I can recall certain occasions when it did *not*. Once there was a puppy Amelia loved, for instance ... it had to be given away; another time, it was a long-anticipated birthday treat that coincided with one of Elizabeth's routs ... and each time she could not face any childish reproaches. It had to appear *my* fault!" He flung his hands apart, saying finally, "Ah, what does it matter, it is all past, dead!"

But he could not, all the same, let matters rest, for he continued sadly, "I need not have been so harsh and intolerant with her ... she was, after all, no different from when I married her, and the fault was mine, in thinking I could change her. I used even to shout at her, you know, and sneer at her foolish little demands, refusing her what I had come to consider her empty pleasures!"

Harriet, remembering her suspicions of physical violence, blushed inwardly for shame, and was indeed, so occupied with self-recrimination that she barely heard Mr. De Brandon continue, almost incuriously, and certainly without rancor. "I wonder who it was she transferred her affections to . . . young Lyndon, perhaps. I collect he was often among our guests in happier days, and always mooning around Elizabeth in a puppy-ish fashion." He continued, on a lower, thoughtful note, "Yes, he is the most likely, now I remember. . . . But he went away just before her death, to visit his father's Continental banking houses, I seem to recall. . . ."

He looked up suddenly at Harriet, his face a mask of pain mingled with pity, "It must have been no accident, but suicide, after all . . . but because of his desertion, perhaps, rather than my—shortcomings." His voice faded. "It is of no consequence now to her, poor child, or to me. And if it was young Lyndon who was her lover, he is punished enough, it would seem, from Amelia's story . . . Best for Elizabeth's sake to inquire no more. . . ."

The silence lengthened again, until Mr. De Brandon moved suddenly, and said, in a far more normal tone of voice, that he did not know what he had been about to so plague her with his affairs, that he was grateful to her for all she had told him, and that he knew he could trust her absolute discretion on the matter. He might, he supposed, contrive to approach Lyndon at some time, if only to set his own mind at rest; but Harriet, anyway, could rest assured that he would do everything to encourage Amelia in her new happiness.

At this, Harriet lifted her head, and gave her warm smile of approval. She was about to continue encouragingly that the child had much to look forward to, when she was unaccountably stopped by Mr. De Brandon moving forward swiftly, and bending his tall figure a little, looking curiously deep into her eyes. She felt her hands taken in a firm clasp, and heard him say, in a low voice and with some hesitancy, "Lady Frome, I have so much to thank you for, not least your resolution and courage in telling me all this. I know I am not the easiest person to deal with—"

He stopped, but whether from diffidence or because another thought had struck him, she knew not, finally continuing, incoherently, "I admire a woman of high courage, of determination. And you, not only with Amelia, but with your brother, too . . . you have had so much to contend with, yet you never complain, never repine, never lose heart . . . I wish, I wish—"

But here he stopped abruptly, and dropping her hands with equal suddenness, said in a totally different, almost disinterested voice, "At what hour do you leave tomorrow?"

Harriet felt an unaccountable stab of chagrin. "As early as I may. The distance is not great, but I fear the roads farther north may be indifferent going—" Suddenly bethinking herself of the need for an escort, she added, "And may I ask your indulgence for a groom to accompany us? John, our second coachman, you know, whom Geoffrey left here, is a sound man, but as there will be but my maid and myself—"

"There is no need of a groom, Lady Frome: I had already decided you could not travel so. I will accompany you."

She surprised herself by saying, in a very decided tone of voice, "No!"

He gave her a wide stare of pure astonishment, causing her to add, more graciously, "I assure you, there is no need—"

"I consider myself to be the better judge of *that*. And it is not my practice to allow females, however self-reliant, to journey about the countryside unattended."

Regarding the stubborn set of Harriet's mouth, he added, in sardonic amusement, "I shall *ride,* Lady Frome, *alongside!* You will not have my company imposed on you."

"There is no question of your company being distasteful, sir. It is just that I prefer to travel alone for"—here her ingenuity failed her; indeed, she could not think why she was so averse to his company, only that this was so, and she added lamely—"for several reasons!"

His expression darkened. "As it is not my company you object to, I can only suppose you are not eager to arrive at your future host's with me in attendance. . . . It would perhaps look odd"—here he mimicked her—" 'for several reasons.' I shall leave you at the Lodge gates." He added, as an apparent casual aside, "Is Sir Henry Bohun to be one of the party?"

This was too much. Harriet's temper rose, and she said acidly, that Sir Henry was not expected at Lord Grafton's but would be anxiously awaiting her return to Surrey, which she intended to make as soon as possible. Especially since, she added, he had very much disliked the idea of her traveling so far afield in the first place, but being a kind and reasonable man, appreciated her sentiments in feeling bound to do so for Geoffrey's sake.

As soon as the words were out, Harriet regretted them. It was ungracious, a deliberate affront to so force her commitment to Sir Henry on Mr. De Brandon's notice. That he was at least affectionately inclined toward her himself she knew; that his offer to accompany her was made out of kindness and a concern for her safety she also realized; she had been very remiss to act so. These self-reprimands had no sooner entered her head than she was about to apologize, but she was forestalled from speaking a word by Mr. De Brandon himself, who remarked, through his teeth, that in that case, there was no more to be said, Lady Frome could go when and where she pleased, and that a woman of such force of character should certainly be proof against the worst of rogues or pickpockets. At this, any thought of apology flew from Harriet's head; indeed, she was hard put to it not to reply to such a remark with all the force of her natural wit. But she refrained, and the two of them stared at each other in utter cold dislike, until Mr. De Brandon moved toward the door, saying languidly that he felt sure she must be fatigued and would want to retire early so as to be ready for her journey tomorrow. Harriet, repressing a childish desire to repudiate any feeling of weariness in order to see how Mr. De Brandon would deal with such insubordination, said distantly that she was, indeed, tired, and walked toward the door which he held open for her. As she passed, he remarked stonily that he presumed she would still do him the honor of accepting his groom, as she had suggested this in the first place, and was not, presumably, so lost to sense that she now intended to refuse this. However coldly put, Harriet realized this to be a sincere offer of help, and a necessity on her part. She therefore accepted his offer with equal coolness, hardly pausing in her walk toward the staircase and Miss Phipps' bedchamber.

Once there, however, she sank down in the basket chair, almost overcome, and thankful that Amelia was sleeping peacefully across the passage. She recalled the tall figure, the dark glance, the shock of revelation Mr.

De Brandon had suffered that very evening, and the final humiliation he had received from her herself. She could at least have spared him that ... she need not have deliberately committed herself to Sir Henry in such a fashion, at such a time. But she *was* so committed, she reasoned; and suddenly, she knew ... she knew why she feared to travel with Mr. De Brandon, why she had made such feeble excuses to avoid doing so, and why her thoughts had been in such a turmoil since his return to Hoyton Hall. She was in love with him, and had been so for a very long time.

With this realization, her thoughts became insupportable, she rose from the chair and walked hastily over to the window, drawing back the curtain, and remembering how he had done so, in great distress only a few hours earlier; she *ought* to have known, she thought bitterly, she was no green girl not to have analyzed her feelings. ... And now, it was too late. But it had long ago been too late, she argued within herself: she had deluded herself, and Sir Henry, that it was him she loved, his kindness, his normality, his resemblance to her first husband ... and there was no going back.

It was as well, she thought bitterly next morning, that she had resigned herself to the inevitable, since any attempt at a rapprochement with Mr. De Brandon was clearly impossible. He did not appear at breakfast, which she took early but with little appetite, having already had a trying and tearful session with poor Amelia. Nor was he to be seen during her farewells to Miss Phipps and the upper servants; indeed, it was only after she had finally kissed Amelia goodbye again, this time standing on the wide steps of the porch; promised once again to ask the Keithleys to invite her to Surrey; and entered the carriage with her abigail, that Mr. De Brandon appeared in the doorway and walked forward to take Amelia's hand.

Gripping the strap with one gloved hand, Harriet raised the other in farewell, and was only just able to see a cold, grave answering salute before the tears filled her eyes, and house, host, and child waved in her vision, disappearing altogether as the carriage swept round the first loop of the driveway.

CHAPTER XVI

It was almost the end of summer. Harriet had long ago come back from Lord Grafton's and after a brief visit to the Keithleys, had returned to Dorking, with Miss Neligan as her constant companion. She had refused Sir Henry; she could not, she realized, support such a marriage, however good and kind and reliable he might be, and it would have been worse than unfair to him, feeling as she did, to embark on such a life. She had seen nothing of Amelia. She had tried writing to invite the child to stay with the Keithleys, for they had been kind enough to offer to have her, or with herself at Dorking. But she had received only a formal note from Mr. De Brandon in reply, saying briefly that he hoped to take Amelia to the Continent for a spell, to help her forget her previous unhappiness and improve her mind, and that therefore it was not possible to accept her kind invitation. There was no mention of a visit at a later date, and Harriet took this, as it was obviously meant, as a desire to break off all communication with Surrey. There was nothing she could do; she regretted the loss of the child's friendship, for Amelia's sake as well as her own, but was sensible enough to realize that Amelia would be content and happy enough in her new-found relationship with her papa; and indeed, that Mr. De Brandon was wise and loving enough to foster that friendship carefully.

Revolving once again all these thoughts in her mind, Harriet sat by the window in her small boudoir, watching the damp mists, presage of autumn, creeping sadly across the dank garden, its grass scattered already with dead leaves, which no amount of sweeping by the gardeners seemed to remove. Inside the room the log fire, however bright, seemed of little avail against the chill that seeped in beneath the window sashes, and when a spatter of rain blew in a sudden shower against the glass, Harriet's low spirits sank even lower. Almost she gave way to despair, but becoming aware of Miss Neligan, apparently engaged with her embroidery frame, but in reality watching her niece narrowly, she rallied and said, with a rather forced gaiety, that she had hoped to see the Keithleys arrive to call this forenoon, but with the sudden rain it must be supposed *that* to be impossible. She added she had some letters to write, however, and would attend to these instead. Miss Neligan was not deceived: with a pronounced sniff, she remarked acidly that if Harriet continued to refuse some friends, and cut herself off from others, she would soon have no one left to write letters to.

Correctly interpreting this to be yet another reference to her refusal of Sir Henry, which her aunt deplored, and which had saddened, and even caused a slight estrangement from, her dear friends the Keithleys, Harriet sighed. She was tired of Surrey, tired of her life there, tired even of Geoffrey, now reestablished at Knoll House and seeming, at present at least, a little more settled and less irresponsible in his behavior. Indeed, the only lightening of her dark horizon was the continuing affection between Selina and Mr. Huntley, their wedding now fixed for next spring, and eagerly anticipated by everyone. Whenever Harriet drove herself over to the Keithleys, which was less frequently than it had used to be, she was heartened by Selina's obvious happiness, and the improvement in her disposition and spirits; it was a relief, a refreshment, to see an affair of the heart turn out so well. . . .

Her letters untouched, she continued brooding in this manner, for once not attempting to rally her spirits, or talk to Miss Neligan, when she heard a carriage draw up despite the rain and Mr. Keithley was announced, with Anne and Selina. Anne, who was expecting her first child within some six months, looked well, her delicate complexion flushed, her pretty auburn hair luxuriant, its tendrils curling crisply in the damp air. Selina, too, was in good looks, and the two of them brought such a breath of well-being and happiness into the room that Harriet could not help but feel her spirits lift.

"We are going to Brighton!" exclaimed Selina, as soon as they were seated, "and we have come *especially,* on such a tiresome wet day, to ask for Miss Neligan and you to accompany us!"

When no one else spoke, she went on, excitedly, "Mr. Huntley is there already, with his parents; indeed, it was their suggestion that we all come down for a short period."

Harriet broke in, a little listlessly, that it was surely too late in the year, and the weather too bad, to think of such an expedition, but at this, speaking above Selina's twitters of disagreement, Edward Keithley remarked calmly, "No, Harriet my dear: September is considered an excellent month in Brighthelmston. Indeed, King George himself is still there, and declares his intention of remaining in that monstrosity of a palace of his until the end of the month, so half the world remains in the town, too. I collect it was the same in previous years, when he was still the Prince Regent."

But Harriet could work up little enthusiasm, even attempting to ignore the hopeful look which always appeared on her aunt's face whenever any kind of jaunt or entertainment was proposed, and pointing out the difficulty, since the town was still so full, of finding lodgings there, especially for so brief a period.

"I declare you are a real killjoy!" exclaimed Selina with more accuracy than manners, and in the high tone she still sometimes employed when disagreed with, "There is *no* difficulty about lodgings, Mr. Huntley says he has some suitable ones provisionally reserved for us—quite elegant, and just off the Steine—which he can hold until next Thursday, the present occupants not leaving until then." She turned to her old ally Miss Neligan, expostulating, "Can *you* do nothing with her, Ma'am? She is become as Gothic as—"

But here she had gone too far, and was reproved by everyone; and on Miss Neligan saying nothing, it was left to Anne to add, with gentle diffidence, "If you really do not wish it, we shall of course not attempt to persuade you. But I should be so glad of your company, Harriet: this is to be my last expedition for some time, you know, since by next month I shall have to lead a quiet life, and put my feet up, and behave in every way like a future mamma!" Here she cast a gentle look at her husband, and received a glance of such love and kindness in return that Harriet's heart ached suddenly. She was moved, too, by Anne's appeal, by her obvious desire for her companionship, and said, spontaneously, "Selina is to the right of it: I am become quite Gothic! Of course I will come; I shall enjoy a change beyond anything. And so will you, Aunt, will you not?"

She was rewarded with such a dazzling smile from Miss Neligan, and such expressions of pleasure from the others, as to put her to shame, and she said, low, to her aunt that she must indeed have been a dreary companion this long time. It was not Miss Neligan's way to deny a truth, but she replied gruffly that Harriet's low spirits were understandable, adding brightly that anyway here was an end to them, and when did the Keithleys intend to leave? An immediate discussion ensued, so that by the end of the morning all necessary arrangements had been agreed upon, and Edward Keithley proposed to send a messenger at once to the Huntleys signifying their intention of joining them in Brighton by the end of the week.

The following Friday, therefore, saw the party arrived in Brighton. The lodgings were found to be excellent, and fashionably close to the Steine; the weather was balmy and sunny; and the town still crowded with the *ton,* the crush in the theaters and Circulating Libraries alone exhilarating to Harriet after her deliberate seclusion in Surrey. Her usual common sense and optimism returned, and she told herself, as she walked the next morning along the Steine with her friends about her, that she must really take herself in hand and repine no more.

This resolve proved not to be difficult. She and the Keithleys were known and greeted by many people, and invitations to card parties, coffee parties, even small routs and balls, began to deluge the pleasant house where they were lodged. Inevitably she experienced a few awkward moments: she came one afternoon upon the Misses Langland who told her, with wide eyes, that they had recently met Sir Henry Bohun in Town, and how sorry they were to find her betrothal to him was no longer to be anticipated. Harriet's first thought, on hearing their chatter, was a vast relief that Sir Henry was in Town and not here in Sussex; her second, what a ninny she had been for it never to have occurred to her that he might have been in Brighton. (On her remarking on this later to Anne, however, Anne had laughed, saying gently that Edward had already discreetly ascertained Sir Henry's plans before suggesting Harriet accompany them; and Harriet was moved afresh by the kindness shown her by all her friends.)

On another occasion she came across Mrs. Wentworth, who was to be seen about with what Harriet and the Keithleys privately were wont to call the vulgar smart set, and here, indeed, she suffered more. She had just entered that fashionable meeting place, Donaldson's Circulating Library, with the intention not of gossiping, but of changing her book while awaiting Anne and Selina, who were gone to the milliner's, when to her acute embarrassment she was hailed in affected tones, and glancing round, saw to her dismay Mrs. Wentworth with a large party assembled in a far corner, the latter waving her hand in its light tan glove, and calling, nodding, and beckoning all at once. There was nothing for it but to go over with as much grace as she could muster, and Harriet did so, noticing, as she went, that all the most malicious tongues, and very little breeding, seemed to be assembled there.

She was right to be apprehensive: a place was quickly made for her, and as she joined the group, Mrs. Wentworth said, in her usual honeyed tones, "How long it is since we have seen you, my dear Lady Frome! I declare you are quite a dark horse, traveling so *very* far north, and leaving so *many* dear friends disconsolate in Surrey. ... And then on your return even, disappearing so completely from all your usual *haunts;* and when we had all such high hopes of something *exciting* being in the wind, too!"

The avid faces around her seemed to resolve into a single bright knowing eye, long nose, and craned neck, but Harriet, although wondering inwardly whether Mrs. Wentworth intended her veiled references to apply to Sir Henry Bohun or to Hugh De Brandon, said calmly enough, "I cannot think why you should have been so preoccupied with my dull affairs, Mrs. Wentworth; for I assure you they *are* dull, so run of the mill that they are not worth a moment's thought, let alone several weeks." She tempered this uncompromising reply with a smile so warm that any sense of offense was, she hoped, removed, while at the same time her would-be tormentor was warned against further discussion of such matters. But this was a vain attempt; Mrs. Wentworth's eyes and teeth flashed again, and she said archly, "Oh come, you are too modest! When two such very difficult gentlemen were always to be seen in your company, and you *defended* the one so gallantly, and were *seen* so often with the other ... well, as my late husband, who was a racing man, would have said, one might almost make a book on it!"

Not for the first time, Harriet felt her breath taken

away by the crass vulgarity of the speaker. She had no
doubt Mrs. Wentworth's reference to a gallant defense
was meant to recall her support of Mr. De Brandon at
Jane Bentley's in Town some time ago, the last occasion,
indeed, that she and Mrs. Wentworth had met. Moreover,
a hasty glance round the sea of interested faces recalled to
her an even earlier scene, in the ballroom at the Hartleys,
when she had so drawn attention to herself in an argument with Mr. De Brandon about Miss Austen, of all
things! However, she allowed not one glimpse of her
dismayed thoughts to appear on her face, and turned
deliberately with a smile to talk to a reasonably harmless
acquaintance on her left. Mrs. Wentworth, recognizing a
temporary defeat, let matters slide for a little, but just as
Harriet was feeling she could, without causing comment,
move to leave, the sharp eyes flashed again, and the honeyed voice rose.

"I was just saying to my friend here—are you acquainted with Mrs. Sargent, Lady Frome?—that Mr. De Brandon would seem at last to be settling down! As I am sure
you know, being so *old* a friend, he returned to England
with his child some weeks ago, and is now quite *épris* with
the daughter of a neighbor of his in Lancashire, a Miss
Melissa Luton. The family do not come much to Town,
but you may know her perhaps from your stay at Hoyton
Hall?"

This was said with deliberate malice, and Harriet could
only shake her head.

"You do *not?* Well, she is so young—almost, one might
say cruelly, *too* young for him—but so beautiful! And we
all know, do we not, how often older, sophisticated men
lose their heads where youth, goodness, and beauty are
concerned? They are often foolish enough to wish to

marry! And the *on-dit* is that this is the case with Mr. De Brandon. Admittedly, he has more reason than most to wish to do so, since Melissa, as well as being such a beautiful, good-natured creature, and clever too, simply *dotes* on Amelia."

This speech showed an insight into Mr. De Brandon's affectionate regard for his daughter, and suggested the speaker to have a knowledge of his character and preferences which was disconcerting. And although aware of Caroline Wentworth's tactics, and determined not to be affected by them, Harriet nevertheless felt a sudden contraction of her heart . . . it was all so possible, nay, extremely likely. She was aware the entire group had suddenly fallen silent, and was lifting her head, attempting to evince such casual interest as would appear she had heard, but not regarded, Mrs. Wentworth's last thrust, when she saw, to her vast relief, Edward Keithley striding across the room toward her. She half turned, and as soon as he was within hearing distance, he said firmly, "Harriet, I am directed to come at once to tell you that Anne and Selina are delayed at the milliner's, a farrago of nonsense about some folderol or other—a bonnet trimmed wrong, I collect! So I am to rescue you from boredom and walk with you back to the house." He added quizzically, "But I conjecture *boredom* would seem hardly the correct word!"

Unavoidably, he met Mrs. Wentworth's eye, and looked away. Harriet rallied. "Oh no, I cannot claim to have been *bored*," she said, smiling warmly all round the circle. "We have had a really pleasant gossip, have we not, and I must thank you for so entertaining me!"

As they left the Library, with apparent goodwill on all sides, Edward asked a little grimly, half jokingly, "And what was all that about? I must say, I cannot admire your choice of friends!"

When there was no reply, he looked kindly down at the bent head, Harriet's face being hidden by a very becoming blue bonnet, and asked gently, "Has that insufferable woman been tormenting you again?"

With such kindly understanding, Harriet, who had been about to relieve her spirits by flaring up and saying that the company had chosen her, rather than her them, said instead very low, "She told me, or as good as, that Hugh De Brandon is returned from the Continent ... and is about to become betrothed, or is even already so, to a Melissa Luton, whose family live in the north of the country."

Mr. Keithley did not speak, and she glanced anxiously up at him, to see a somewhat puzzled compassion in his grave regard. He answered slowly, "I do not really know, Harriet, how much truth there is to this. I was in my club the other day, and met a fellow member whom both De Brandon and I know reasonably well. ... He—did mention something of De Brandon seeming to be 'caught at last,' as I believe he put it. But whether that was just one of his usual racy figures of speech, or something more certain, I have no idea."

He went on, with some concern, and very gently, "Does it mean so much to you, my dear?"

But Harriet could not answer him at once; she had to dig her nails into the palms of her hands through her gloves, and swallow hard, before she could say, with reasonable aplomb, "No, of course not! It is just that I am a little surprised ... but if she is so nice a girl, and fond of Amelia, it would be the best thing in the world for all three of them!"

She had no means of knowing if Edward was really satisfied with this answer or not. But he appeared to be, and indeed, she told herself, there was no reason why he should not be; so the subject was dropped, and the two of them walked back along the Steine together, Harriet chattering as though she had not a thought above the week's entertainment in her mind.

CHAPTER XVII

During the following week, everyone remarked on how dazzling Lady Frome had suddenly become; invariably amusing, always in good looks, these personal advantages seemed suddenly heightened, drawing even more admiring glances than usual, so that where before she was everywhere welcomed, her presence was now, as it were, essential for the ensured success of any party. Those few close and dear to her, admittedly, felt a little uncomfortable that, where her brilliance had increased, something of her real kindness had been lost, but all the same her sympathy and good nature were so inherent in her that no one actually suffered from what it was hoped must be the temporary eclipse of a deeper warmth.

One forenoon toward the weekend, then, with but two more weeks of the visit to Brighton remaining, she was hurrying along the Steine, having just drunk chocolate with a particularly amusing group of friends, when across the road, near the square where her lodgings were situated, she became aware of a figure standing regarding her. Something in its absolute immobility among the fashionable crowds who thronged the pavements had drawn her eyes in the first place, and now, at a second glance, she recognized Mr. De Brandon. Her consternation and dismay were extreme, but as she hesitated, the figure moved suddenly, crossing the road to where she stood irresolute. He was in front of her before she had time to collect her wits, but it seemed he suffered no similar sense of embarrassment, for he bowed and put out his hand to hers, saying in pleasantly languid tones, "Lady Frome! I had not thought to meet you here, imagining you to be snug in Surrey!"

Somehow she contrived to smile, and keeping her voice as casual as his own, explained she had come at the request of the Keithleys, and was vastly enjoying herself. There was an awkward pause. The breeze had whipped a delicate color into her cheeks, and blown her shining hair, confined by her bonnet, into a slight disarray that was wholly charming. Although caused by embarrassment, and illogical annoyance at his composure, her brown eyes had a sparkle in their velvet depths and this, together with the natural warmth of her regard, made her well nigh irresistible. Her dove gray walking habit, too, rather severe in cut, increased her air of delicate distinction: indeed, she had never looked so fine, Hugh De Brandon was aware of it, and she in her turn, like any pretty woman, sensed his admiration. Suddenly the world appeared a far less drab place than it had seemed to her in her secret heart and, following her natural kind inclination, she asked how

Amelia did. At this, Mr. De Brandon's austere expression relaxed into enthusiasm, and he explained that she was well, indeed seemed quite cured of her earlier maladies, and was at present staying with some young friends in London.

"I cudgeled my brains, you know, Lady Frome, and realized on reflection that I still had *some* acquaintances, though admittedly from many years ago, who had married and lived comfortably, and were proud parents to children of Amelia's age, so I revived our friendship for her sake!"

This was said so easily, and with the implication that it was Harriet's advice which had originally put him in mind of such a move, that Harriet felt her earlier restraint vanish. She was happy both for him and for Amelia, and said so sincerely, inviting him, at the same time, to accompany her to her lodgings, as she knew both Anne and Mr. Keithley to be at home. Mr. De Brandon accepted, and the next half-hour was spent companionably with Anne and Edward, everyone appearing to be remarkably at ease, and on the best of terms. At the end of this period, Mr. De Brandon took his leave with perfect equanimity, appearing to hold Harriet, Anne, and Edward in equal regard . . . and Harriet, who had, almost without being aware of doing so, looked for some hint of warmth, some sign of former attachment, had to admit there was none. She realized his feelings for her were without doubt quite gone, and that she would do well to come to terms with this discovery as quickly as possible.

It was no very happy realization, and dressing to attend a musical evening at the house of acquaintances in the neighboring square, Harriet's spirits fell once again. Moreover, they rallied hardly at all on her arrival there, on discovering Hugh De Brandon to be one of the guests, especially when an unknown female seated next to her in the salon where the entertainment was to take place had pointed him out to her, in the flat tones of the North, as a rather distant neighbor "who, we have heard, is to be betrothed to *another* neighbor, a sweet young girl hardly out of her teens!" This was too much; Harriet's somewhat frenetic gaiety deserted her utterly, and she spent a miserable initial hour listening to an indifferent string quartet, and only wishing she were home, and in bed. During an intermission in the concert, however, she was surprised to have Mr. De Brandon seek her out, this time bearing ratafia, cakes, and an invitation to a chair he had reserved for her in a pleasant alcove, since he wished, he explained as soon as they were settled in comparative seclusion, to tell her about Mr. Lyndon. It reflected Harriet's state of mind that she did not at once realize *who* this Mr. Lyndon was, until recalled by Mr. De Brandon to the knowledge that he was the man he had suspected of being Elizabeth's lover. She was horrified at such a lapse of memory, which she had been totally unable to conceal from her companion, but was exonerated by Mr. De Brandon, who said, casually, "No, I beg you, Lady Frome, why should you be expected to remember! I but wished to tell you that I was right in one surmise, and Mr. Lyndon was her would-be lover . . . I called on him, making it clear, as soon as I had discreetly ascertained that he had had at least some interest in her, that I wished the matter forgot, but for my own peace of mind would prefer to know how matters had stood between them at the time. . . . He was almost overcome, and distinctly uneasy," continued Mr. De Brandon with a cold, reminiscent smile, "but he was man enough to tell me everything."

Here, he looked away, being perhaps not as disinterested as he would have Harriet suppose, and continued, distantly, "They had thought themselves to be in love for a long time. . . . God knows how she represented me and her life at Hoyton Hall to him, but she seems to have exaggerated as usual. . . . Anyway, it seems that ultimately, he attempted to persuade her to elope with him. It would appear she must have had some scruples, for she hung back, blew first hot, then cold, until he felt, he told me, almost out of patience with her himself, and issued an ultimatum! He was, he said, leaving next day for Paris to attend to matters at one of his father's banking houses there, and would contrive to wait for her secretly in a discreet closed carriage from an hour before midnight until one o'clock, on the highway behind Hoyton Hall, before driving on southward to take the packet boat to the Continent. If she was not there by one of the clock, he would assume she had rejected him, and leave without her. To make everything easy for her, he told her to bring no valise, nothing, merely wear her everyday clothes and a warm cloak and bonnet, and he would secretly pack some of his sister's things to suffice her until they reached Paris. . . ."

There was another long pause. Until at last Mr. De Brandon continued, in that same dry, seemingly disinterested tone, "Well, she did not come. He waited a full hour longer than he had said, in the hopes that she had merely been delayed . . . and when she had still not appeared, he assumed neither her love nor her nerve to have been strong enough, and left." He added swiftly, "It seems unlikely to have been suicide, therefore, since she would certainly feel, in her foolishly romantic mind, that she had everything to live for. ... We think, Lyndon and I, that she fell on that treacherous cliff road."

Both of them remained silent, visualizing Elizabeth already dead after missing her footing on the cliff path leading toward the highroad, while her lover waited in vain some quarter of a mile distant. At last Mr. De Brandon finished quietly, "It seems that from Paris he went to Rome in unhappy despair and disappointment, from Rome to Geneva, and from there even further afield to Prussia, where he remained for some time. He never knew what had happened to her, only assuming her to have remained with me. Indeed, it was only this year, on his return to England and the North, that he wandered into the rose garden—whether in the hope of seeing her or merely reliving memories I know not, and came upon our Amelia, who told him the story. ..."

He laughed, and added in a casual, hard voice, "Poor fellow, one is almost sorry for him! At least I cannot work up any dire malice against him. And he seems happy enough now, with a gentle creature as a wife, and no terrible passion to contend with. ... We all come to it, I suppose!"

Harriet, taking this remark as a reference to his own attachment to Melissa Luton, was inwardly quite overset, and could do no more than give a nod of agreement to his philosophizing.

She could now hardly wait to return to Surrey. All her newfound content in the friendships and amusements which Brighton had offered incomprehensively vanished; her head ached continuously, the side glances of the gossips seemed directed at her alone, and even the normally happy tenor of life among her own close friends became well nigh insupportable. Indeed, she could not even sum-

mon up any enthusiasm for the highlight of the end of the
Brighton Season, a final glittering ball given by George IV
himself, in his exotic, onion-topped, incredible Royal
Pavilion off the Steine. All the world had been contriving
for cards of invitation, and it was flattering that Edward
Keithley, without any effort on his part, had been among
the first to receive such an invitation for himself and his
party, but Harriet felt no satisfaction in this, although she
did her best to appear delighted. She advised Selina on
her coiffure, suggesting she dress it with a delicate garland
of rosebuds rather than an ornate filet she had inherited
from her mamma; and helped Anne to choose a gown
flattering to her figure, which was already not as slender
as it had used to be. For herself, she dressed languidly,
her boxes already packed for the imminent journey back
to Surrey, and her thoughts already far away from
Brighton.

CHAPTER XVIII

However Harriet might feel about the occasion, and however uncaringly she had dressed for it, she looked wholly charming. Being at an age where any gaucheries of extreme early womanhood had been refined away, yet possessed of a clear, beautiful skin, fine eyes, heavy luxuriant hair, and a slender figure, she unconsciously presented an appearance that the frequently unformed, rounded features of the younger women could not compete with. Her expression, her bearing, her every gesture, bespoke a refinement of beauty, in body and in mind, and indeed, the King himself, still a connoisseur of womanhood, was swift to notice this, singling her out almost to the point of embarrassment. His stays creaking, his handsome features now somewhat raddled, and his former healthy color turned to a rather unhealthy crimson, he led her out in the ballroom, offered his arm to escort her to the supper room, and finally insisted on showing her his fine collection of Chinese porcelain. This last move, especially, caused her some qualms, as it was generally known that on such occasions his advances often passed beyond the bounds of propriety. But a refusal was impossible, and under the eyes of everyone, therefore, amused, curious, scornful, envious, according to the sex and character of their owners, Harriet accompanied her royal host toward the rooms housing his collection. She found she had misjudged him: although at first, admittedly, attempting to flirt outrageously with her, holding her waist tightly, and essaying to kiss her neck in a very familiar fashion, when she demured, he immediately desisted, saying in a good-naturedly rueful fashion that he was not as young nor as attractive to the fair sex as he had used to be. This made Harriet laugh; and when she explained that neither youth nor attraction had anything to do with her attitude, it was merely that she preferred wit to passion, and conversation to philandering, he smiled very kindly, and sitting down some distance away from her now, on a long, intricately carved sofa, began to talk, as he could on occasion, with brilliance and charm.

In this mood, she found His Majesty interesting and thoroughly likable, and the time passed pleasantly for both of them without their being aware of it. At last, however, her eye fell on the delicate Sèvres timepiece fashionably wrought *à la chinoise,* and rising with an involuntary exclamation, she said she must rejoin her friends. Prinny, as some of his old friends still called him, looked at her regretfully, and observed that doubtless her dearest suitor was become restless, adding a little regretfully that alas, nowadays he had no such companion to watch him with jealous eyes. This statement so accorded with Harriet's own case and state of mind that, with the ease of friendship which the last half-hour had given her, she said impulsively that, alas, matters stood the same with her. The King looked at her consideringly, wholly serious, and observed that surely this could not be so; either she was an unconscionable flirt, which he knew not to be the case, or she was disappointed in love, feeling an affection for someone which was not returned, or at least not to the same degree.

Strangely moved, she admitted to it, whereupon His Majesty, taking her hand in the kindest fashion, said with utter sincerity and conviction, "Do not be too proud, my dear. If you let your pride and your temper rule your actions in such a matter, you will have a whole life to regret it. The object of an attachment, an affection, as intense and warm as yours must surely be is worth fighting for, at least." He smiled suddenly, and added dryly, "So my advice to you is, unless he is already married, abroad, dead, or otherwise unobtainable, swallow your female pride and *encourage* him a little!"

Aware of the gentleness of expression, the sincerity, the vulnerability of the eyes regarding her, she realized suddenly what Maria Fitzherbert had seen in the slowly aging roué, which had enabled her to bear with him through all his vagaries, and all the insults and affronts he had offered her. She said with simplicity, "You are very kind, Sire, to take such an interest ... and I will, I promise you, bear your advice in mind!"

The audience, as it were, being now obviously concluded, the two of them strolled, very amicably, back to the public rooms, King George to wander over to his cronies again, occasionally ogling a pretty face, and Harriet

to pick up the threads of her evening as best she might.
She was uncomfortably aware of being the most interesting topic of conversation and speculation in the room,
and that the experienced eyes of sophisticates and gossips
alike were directed on her in varying degrees of discretion. She could only be thankful that Mrs. Wentworth and
some of her companions had been considered too inferior
for invitations to be sent them; but since others of her
friends, of perhaps higher rank but equal vulgarity of
spirit, were present, she felt relieved that within two days
she would have left Brighton and be quit of such constant
speculative stares.

Anne and Edward Keithley, and others of their party,
formed a protective enough cover for her, however, and
she was able, during a cotillion, to calm Edward Keithley's
fears that she had found herself in some difficulties. With
such concern, and later the amused interest of her friends
to allay and satisfy, however, her mind was at least dis-
tracted from her earlier miserable loneliness, so that it
was with less extreme feelings that she eventually came
face to face with Mr. De Brandon during one of the country dances George IV was still so fond of. Holding her
fingertips in the correct fashion as they sidestepped down
the room, he asked her lightly and somewhat sardonically,
but without any intent to give offense, if she had had an
interesting audience with His Majesty. At this Harriet,
remembering her conversation with the King, and the subject of his concluding advice, was hard put to it not to
laugh, albeit a little bitterly, and tell Mr. De Brandon,
without reference to personalities, what she and King
George had ultimately spoken of. She controlled herself,
however, merely remarking, with truth, that she had
nothing to complain of in His Majesty's conduct, he had

behaved in a very proper manner, as well as proving an interesting conversationalist.

She spoke with such underlying amusement, and with such a, now, unfamiliar hint of high spirits, that Mr. De Brandon was intrigued in spite of himself. This annoyed him, for he had been doing his best, during his Continental tour and after his return to England, to forget Harriet. He had told himself continually that she was affianced to Sir Henry, and when, recently, he had discovered this not to be so, had attempted to convince himself that her independent manner, and what he chose to call, once again, her interfering ways, were best avoided anyway: he would, he had vowed, never become involved with her again.

A chance meeting on the Steine had, indeed, renewed their acquaintanceship, but at that time Mr. De Brandon had felt perfectly safe in his resolution. It was only as the days passed that he had begun to feel his resolve gradually slipping away: she was to be met with everywhere, and everywhere her niceness of character, as well as her warmth and beauty, was revealed, often in the smallest of ways, and despite her heightened and wholly fascinating wit and charm. In vain did he attempt to conjure up the image of young and gentle Melissa Luton, whose name the gossips, he knew, were already coupling with his own (though without any real reason, since they were but friends and he had never led her to expect any declaration, *her* indifference to any advances and *his* memory of his first marriage being powerful deterrents to his doing so). Now, Harriet's face, Harriet's conversation, Harriet's character, would keep intervening in his thoughts and disturbing his peace of mind; indeed, he had been surprised, this very evening, at the knot of angry dismay within him

when he saw her so pointedly the object of the King's gal-
lantries. He was recalling again that unexpected sensation,
and speaking hardly at all, when, having reached the head
of the set, he must separate from her, with nothing said
except banalities, and nothing further to bring them together again for the rest of the evening, since he was with
one party, she with another. . . . He walked off the floor at
the conclusion of the dance with his dark, closed look on
his face, causing Harriet, who could not help but watch
him surreptitiously, to reflect bitterly that he was a very
sour and moody man, after all, and it was as well she was
quite rid of him.

This thought, however, gave her no satisfaction, and
desiring nothing better, for the moment, than to be alone,
she exclaimed at the heat, excused herself from her
friends, and went to walk in the Chinese Gallery, now
near empty, since the reception was long over. It was cool
here, and quieter, with so few people about that she could
imagine herself solitary, so wishing nothing better than to
be home in bed, but unable to spoil the enjoyment of the
others by so selfishly declaring this, Harriet sat down and
became occupied with her thoughts. After a little while
the gallery emptied completely, the strains of the waltz
drawing everyone toward the great ballroom again. This
dance, which the King, as Prinny, had sanctioned with his
usual boldness years ago, had remained extremely popular, only a few elderly people still choosing to look on
with disapproval. So it was that Harriet, now quite solitary, clearly heard soft footsteps approaching her down
the long room. She glanced up; and there stood Mr. De
Brandon before her, with a strange look of uncertainty
and, almost, truculence on his dark handsome face.

He said abruptly, in a manner hardly calculated to please, "It is no use, I have tried to avoid our paths continuously crossing, but it has proved impossible."

Harriet felt a stir of resentment now, added to her sense of listless misery, and replied, in a deliberate cool manner, her voice very light, "I cannot think why you should have gone to such trouble; was it for my convenience, or your own, that you attempted to prevent our meeting so frequently?"

"For both our sakes," answered Mr. De Brandon harshly. He then burst out, uncontrollably, "You have a—a fascination for people that is wholly absorbing. And misleading. One comes to think of you as a kindred spirit, and with a wholehearted interest in one's affairs, whereas—" Here he broke off, aware perhaps that in speaking with such frankness he was also being excessively and rudely critical. But Harriet's quick temper had again claimed her, and she asked, with misleading calm, "Whereas instead?"

"Instead, you are merely curious, and thoughtlessly kind. You must always be knowing the how, and the why, people behave as they do, but are never concerned with the *effect* your interest may have on those people. . . . Oh, you are good-natured, I admit, but never truly kind, never thinking to consider how your early warmth may affect people's lives, or your later disinterest and withdrawal from their affairs may distress them, when you have found some other interest, or cause, to embrace!"

This was so unjust, or at least so mistaken a judgment, that poor Harriet's eyes filled with tears. She did not let them be seen, however, merely sat, seemingly indifferent, without speaking. She heard Mr. De Brandon continue very low, still apparently unable to stop himself, "Do you remember last spring? When we first met, you fascinated me, and as I came to *imagine* I knew you better, I began to hold you in very high esteem. I was foolish enough to think, from your manner, that your sentiments were, perhaps, similar to mine, and for the first time in two years, I let down my guard, and allowed my feelings a little rein. ... But then, you may recall, there came the Hartleys' ball: I was sure, early that evening, that with time you might come to—to have an affection for me, and I was foolish enough to feel *elated*." His dark countenance flushed, and his mouth twisted bitterly. "But *that very same night* I find you equally engrossed with some other poor fool at your feet." He went on. "I could understand if after a *period of time* you found yourself to be mistaken in your feelings of affinity, and your manner toward me changed accordingly, but a brief *hour or so* is insupportable!"

This further injustice goaded Harriet to a deep, cold anger, and she said through her teeth, "You are too hasty in your opinions and judgments, Sir. What you interrupted and chose—I beg pardon, *choose*—to regard as a light-hearted thoughtless conquest by a—an inquisitive flirt—was in fact a rejection of an extremely gentle and kind suitor!"

She looked him full in the face then, her beautiful eyes appearing even more dazzling by reason of the tears sparkling there. But Mr. De Brandon merely answered, with a hard stare, and in a deliberate impersonal tone, "Oh come, Lady Frome! You soon became as good as betrothed to the gentleman ... and then later you abandoned him, too, poor fellow."

Harriet could not bring herself to point out this further unjust and incorrect interpretation of her actions, and would certainly not explain to the disdainful, conceited, and selfish creature before her that *he* was the reason both for her earlier turning toward Sir Henry and her later refusal of him. She rose without a word, therefore, and walked away down the gallery; and Mr. De Brandon, wishful to follow her, yet held back by his anger and resentment, watched her graceful figure slowly move away from him without a backward glance.

The following morning, after an unhappy and sleepless night, Harriet found herself with no further time to brood. Anne's present physical state was causing her to feel rather poorly, and in need of rest; Miss Neligan, perhaps because of sitting in a draught at the pavilion the previous evening, was also indisposed; and Selina was indulging in one of her now mercifully rare bouts of ill temper, her fiancé having broken an engagement to take her driving that morning since his father urgently required his presence at home on some matter of business. With only Edward Keithley and herself, therefore, to arrange for their departure the next day, and with invalids and ill temper to contend with, Harriet found her hands very full indeed, even despite Anne's gentle attempts to help, and Miss Neligan's brave insistence that she needed no cosseting. She was just hurrying along the upper hall, having herself prepared a special tisane for her aunt, when the bell clanged, a servant could be heard admitting a visitor, and in no time Harriet was told that Mr. De Brandon was below, asking for her.

It was in her mind to refuse him, saying she was not at

home, but feeling this would but play into his hands, and increase his conviction that he was correct in his unjust estimation of her character by showing herself to be resentful, ungracious, and high-handed, she hurried down to the salon, intent on begging him to state his business and release her to her many duties as quickly as possible.

On her arrival, however, she found him to be in a state of great perturbation: he turned from the bay window, where he had been pacing up and down, and came across to her, saying hurriedly, distractedly, and with none of his usual languid, sardonic undertones, "Lady Frome, I collect you leave tomorrow, and must therefore have much in hand today, but I could not let you go without offering my sincerest, my most abject, apologies for my behavior last night!" He continued, with difficulty, "It was inexcusable; prejudiced, hurtful—I cannot account for it. At least, I beg you, say you will but attempt to forgive me, and I shall not disturb you further!"

Remembering her wakeful night, and if the truth be known, the tears she had shed, her constant profitless refining on her life, her ways, her friendships, her responsibilities, Harriet could feel now nothing but bitter anger. That he should first so insult and hurt her; and then ease his conscience by arriving, at what he knew to be an impossible time, to ask her forgiveness! She said, with deliberate indifference that of course he was forgiven, and it was anyway no great matter, since his opinion of her was not like to cast her into a decline.

"If we took to heart the thoughtless, ill-judged criticisms of every ill-informed or ill-natured acquaintance, Mr. De Brandon, we should all soon be in the suds of despair. Besides, you must not distress yourself unduly: with my *shallow* emotions it is quite impossible for me to be much hurt or deeply angered, and I can therefore forgive as lightly, with the same shallow, facile ease."

She smiled with deliberate false sweetness at his aghast expression, and concluded briskly, "And now, if you will excuse me, I must go and *interfere* with the affairs of this household. I have great scope for my organizing powers today, and am *curious* to see how I can deal with my problems. There is Anne, indisposed and tearful; and when I have *tired* of comforting her, I can go and ask the *how's* and *why's* of my aunt, who is sick of a bad cold, an indisposition not to be taken lightly at her age; and finally I can try my hand at *charming* Selina out of a sad fit of the sulks. . . . Well, that is not quite the final enjoyment in store for me for, would you believe it, I have the preparations for leaving tomorrow to attend to as well—I can oversee the packing, and make sure that Miss Neligan's vinaigrette and hot bricks are left available for the journey, and organize the servants, and check the linen—oh, there are a million things to be organized and interfered with!"

She held out her hand with the same false charm to him, and as he took it instinctively, staring at her, concerned and wholly discomfited, she attempted to withdraw her fingers again at once, intent only on escaping from the room. But his hand tightened over hers, and he immediately began to say, with such feeling that she could not interrupt, or even continue her attempt to withdraw her hand from his, "Oh no, you must not let my cruel misrepresentations so overset you! I have no right to cause you such distress! I *know*—who could not, after talking with your graceless brother—that your whole life has been one long battle to serve your family: first, to comfort your

mother and wait upon your father; afterward continually
to defend your brother and protect him from his own
foolishnesses; at present, although she has my deepest respect in that she will not let you *immolate* yourself for her
also, you are constantly attending your elderly aunt's
needs; and soon you will be at Mrs. Keithley's gentle beck
and call. . . . I beg of you, my dear Harriet, for once consider yourself! Say what you wish of me, I have earned
your dislike and contempt, but at least take my advice
and escape such involvements before it is too late. . . .
And tell me you have not taken my harsh words to heart.
I know they are unjust!"

Harriet, sensible only that he had, seemingly without
knowing it, used her Christian name, and with such
warmth, could not answer him. It was too late; he had
demoralized her utterly, and the fact that he could be so
cruel had killed all her previous affection for him. She
could once have loved him. . . . At this point in her
thoughts, she found her hand released, and turned away
from him immediately, to walk toward the door. And then
suddenly, unaccountably, she recalled the gentle, experienced eyes, the raddled features, of King George, and
remembered his advice, and the sober tone in which it
had been delivered. She stopped, and turning impulsively
to Mr. De Brandon, attempted to assure him that he was
sincerely forgiven, and apologize, in her turn, for her own
recent words. Somehow, she found herself explaining that
it was because she had indeed begun to reciprocate his
feelings that she had felt so bitter when he had made his
hasty and incorrect interpretation of her relationship with
Sir Henry. But she did not get far in her explanation: Mr.
De Brandon's tall figure came toward her, she felt his

arms close about her, and then his lips on hers. After a long moment, she rested her head against him, felt his hand gently stroking her hair, and knew that, at last, she was utterly happy.

CHAPTER XIX

It is often the case that when anybody experiences some sudden happiness, whatever it may be, their joy and pleasure react upon people around them, creating a genuine sense of well-being. Harriet's happiness carried her up the stairs to Anne, who on hearing her surprising news immediately felt less weary and depressed; and on to Miss Neligan, whose sore throat and congested lungs seemed to ease miraculously almost at once; and finally, Selina chancing to enter at that moment, even her ill humor faded against the radiant happiness of her older friend. At Edward Keithley's suggestion, and with the landlord's pleased agreement (for the Season was over and an extended rent not to be despised), the party's departure was delayed for some days so that Miss Neligan could be quite recovered, and Harriet and Hugh De Brandon persuaded down from the heights of their new-found pleasure in each other's company, to talk sensibly of announcements and arrangements generally. This in fact took but little time, since they were quickly agreed on a very brief formal announcement in the *Gazette,* a short betrothal, and a pleasant but unspectacular wedding, for they felt that both of them, in their different fashions, had caused comment and gossip enough already.

"Just think how Mrs. Wentworth will enjoy herself! She will dine out on her acquaintanceship, and her prognostications, for weeks!" said Harriet, laughing. But this put her in mind of someone else, and she said anxiously, "But how dreadful, I had quite forgot Melissa Luton. . . . Is it true what is said, that she is *éprise* of you . . . and will she be hurt and quite overset?"

But Mr. De Brandon said quietly, and with utmost sincerity, that Harriet need have no fear for Melissa. *He* had perhaps felt himself a little attracted to her, but there had never been any likelihood of her reciprocating his feelings: that was all the gossips' doing. Indeed, she had even become rather annoyed recently at the couplings of their names when it came to her notice, since she was privately seriously interested in a young man far closer to her in years. He went on to say how happy Amelia would be at the news (for she still asked often after Harriet and was ever hopeful to see her), and added that if Harriet were agreeable, they would visit Amelia at once on their arrival in London, to tell her their news before it became generally known by public announcement. This, too, was readily agreed upon, everyone feeling the happier to know both Amelia and Melissa would be pleased and content at such a betrothal, and that no sensibilities would be hurt. Matters being now arranged to the satisfaction of all,

Hugh De Brandon announced his intention of taking Harriet for a long drive in the surrounding countryside, followed by a very public walk along the Steine, to prepare the hard core of the gossips, who still hung on in the town until His Majesty's departure on the morrow, for the announcement they were soon to read. For it would not be fair, he opined, to spring such a betrothal upon them without their having had a chance to whisper a little behind their fans first!

So Harriet and Mr. De Brandon set out, an elegant couple in an elegant open carriage, to drive along the Steine and on out to the Devil's Dike, and set fashionable tongues wagging every inch of the way.

ABOUT THE AUTHOR

JOAN MELLOWS was born in the north of England, and loves the Lake District, although her parents moved south when she was very young. She read English at Oxford, and spent some time as an advertising copywriter before her marriage. Since then she, her husband who works for an oil company, and later their two children, have been constantly on the move, living in various countries, including Nigeria, the U.S.A., France, and Zaire. During these postings she enjoyed several jobs, including lecturing, publicity, and working in a law library, but did not try her hand at her first novel until four years ago during a brief stay in England, with her son away at Sherborne School, her daughter at Edinburgh University, and time on her hands. The only member of the family who was not surprised at the novel's acceptance was the family Bassett, a hound of such personality that friends acknowledge him first, and whoever he has attached to his lead, later. Joan Mellows now has three novels published, and another in hand.

Victoria Holt

Over 20,000,000 copies of Victoria Holt's novels are in print. If you have missed any of her spellbinding bestsellers, here is an opportunity to order any or all direct by mail.

☐	BRIDE OF PENDORRIC	22870-3	1.75
☐	THE CURSE OF THE KINGS	Q2215	1.50
☐	THE HOUSE OF A THOUSAND LANTERNS	X2472	1.75
☐	THE KING OF THE CASTLE	X2823	1.75
☐	KIRKLAND REVELS	X2917	1.75
☐	LEGEND OF THE SEVEN VIRGIN	X2833	1.75
☐	LORD OF THE FAR ISLAND	22874-6	1.95
☐	MENFREYA IN THE MORNING	23076-7	1.75
☐	MISTRESS OF MELLYN	23124-0	1.75
☐	ON THE NIGHT OF THE SEVENTH MOON	X2613	1.75
☐	THE QUEEN'S CONFESSION	X2700	1.75
☐	THE SECRET WOMAN	X2665	1.75
☐	SHADOW OF THE LYNX	X2727	1.75
☐	THE SHIVERING SANDS	22970-X	1.75

Buy them at your local bookstores or use this handy coupon for ordering:

FAWCETT PUBLICATIONS, P.O. Box 1014, Greenwich Conn. 06830

Please send me the books I have checked above. Orders for less than 5 books must include 60c for the first book and 25c for each additional book to cover mailing and handling. Orders of 5 or more books postage is Free. I enclose $_____ in check or money order.

Mr/Mrs/Miss_____

Address_____

City_____ State/Zip_____

Please allow 4 to 5 weeks for delivery. This offer expires 6/78.

A-3